DIRTY BALLISTICS

SPECIAL WEAPONS & TACTICS 2

PEYTON BANKS

CONTENTS

"Where there is love there is life."

— **Mahatma Gandhi**

1

Aspen Hale stared across the desk at the U.S. Marshall and felt defeated. His eyes met hers, revealing the pity she knew he felt deep down inside.

"So you are telling me that even after I testify against him, I can't go back to my old life?"

Her heart pounded as she stared at the federal agent who she met with weekly in her new city. Columbia, South Carolina, was a long way away from where she grew up, and it looked like she was going to be getting real comfortable in the southern city.

"Unfortunately, people who enter into the witness protection program, we highly advise that they don't go back to their previous lives," U.S. Marshall Elliot Ball announced. He shook his head and leaned back in his chair.

"But that seems a little unfair." She gasped. "I didn't do anything wrong! I've been working with the FBI diligently, and this is the thanks I get?"

"It's never fair, Ms. Hale." He shook his head again.

She still had to get used to the new last name. Aspen pulled in a deep breath and tried to keep the tears from falling. Her life had been ripped away from her, all because of someone else's crooked ways. At least the witness protection program allowed her to keep some form of her identity.

Her first name.

Everything else had been taken from her. The job she loved. Her family. Her friends.

Everything was just...gone.

Instead, here she was, hidden away, living the life of one Aspen Hale.

"Most people who enter the witness protection program are criminals, but you"—he paused and ran a hand through his hair as his tired eyes connected with hers—"you were an innocent who was in the wrong place at the wrong time."

"I know." She sighed. It wasn't fair for her to take her frustrations out on him. He was protecting her and keeping her alive. "Same time and place next week?"

"Yes. You have a good chunk, and try making a friend or two," he advised, standing from behind the desk.

Like that would solve my problem.

She gave him a tight smile as she turned and

walked out. She strode through the building that housed his makeshift office and stepped outside.

Taking a deep breath, she looked around the small downtown and took it all in. This was her life now. She glanced down at her watch—it was time for her to start making her way to work.

She guessed she should be happy that they'd placed her in South Carolina. At least the weather was always nice. They could have placed her in some tiny town in the middle of nowhere Montana. And at least Columbia was a southern city where the people all smiled and had manners.

She began the route to the library where she currently held a job. It didn't pay nowhere near the money she had made in her other life, but it provided a roof over her head.

Before her life had been ripped away, she'd been a successful forensic accountant. The best, and that was what had led to her current life now. Her father, Mason Irwin, was a successful computer tycoon who ran a Fortune 500 company in California. He had become suspicious of some dealings that had been going on with the company and had hired her to look into where money had been disappearing.

Aspen had never wanted run the business but knew that one day she would inherit a hefty sum of money from her parents. Thanks to her father's success, she had never wanted for anything except to make her own way in life. She didn't want to succeed based on her last name. No, Aspen Irwin wanted to make it because of her own hard work.

Once Mason was ready to retire, the board would pick his successor. Yes, her father had tried to groom Aspen and wanted her to be the one who took over, but that just wasn't her. She preferred to be behind the scenes of a business, and numbers were more her thing.

She remembered the day she had discovered that her father had been correct. Someone had been embezzling money from the business, and she couldn't believe who it was.

"Good morning," a voice called out, breaking into Aspen's trip down memory lane.

She glanced up. A woman waved to her from in front of the coffee shop. Aspen returned the smile and waved back. She'd seen and spoken to her a few times when she'd run over to grab a cup of joe. It was a nice, small shop with delicious coffee.

"Good morning," she replied, and for the life of her, she couldn't remember her name, but it didn't stop the lady from offering a bright smile.

This was certainly the south.

Aspen glanced around and found herself in front of the County Library. She took in the stone building that had been around forever and was full of rich history. A deep sigh escaped her chest, and she hefted her purse on her shoulder and hurried into the building.

She was Aspen Hale now.

Library assistant.

"You're early," a familiar voice rang out as she marched into the break room. Her one friend, Evelyn Hayes, was sitting at the table drinking coffee.

"Hey, Evie." She smiled and walked over to her locker. "How's it been today?"

"Quiet, as usual. So, did you think about it?" Evie asked, hope lining her voice.

Without turning around, Aspen knew that her friend would be bouncing in her chair. For weeks now, Evie had been trying to arrange a blind date for Aspen with her neighbor. Aspen had tried to avoid the subject. She'd had too much on her mind to think of dating.

Things like testifying against her father's best friend and partner and staying alive.

"I don't know, Evie," she groaned, securing her belongings up in her locker. She turned and leaned her back against it to stare at Evie.

"Oh, come on. I'm not saying you have to marry him." Evie jumped up from her chair and rushed toward Aspen. "It would just be a date. I think you two would be perfect together."

"How do you know that? We've only been friends for a few months." Aspen chuckled. She'd moved to Columbia a little over three months ago and had been working at the library less than that.

"I have an eye for this sort of thing." Evie shrugged her shoulder.

"Well, if he's so sexy and good-looking, why aren't you dating him?" She cocked an eyebrow and crossed her arms in front of her chest. She'd never had to have anyone arrange a date for her before and she wouldn't be starting now. It wasn't that she was vain about her appearance, but she knew she was blessed in the looks department.

"He's not my type," she replied matter-of-factly. "But you two would make a perfect couple."

"What's wrong with him if he can't get a date himself?" Something had to be wrong with the guy. A sexy man never needed help finding a woman. If he was as good-looking as Evie gushed, something had to be wrong with him.

"I promise. There is nothing wrong with Declan. Pinkie swear." Evie offered her pinky to Aspen. Her friend was vastly growing on her, and Aspen knew she meant well.

Try making a friend or two, the words of Agent Ball rang in her head.

Well, if it didn't work out between her and this Declan, she could always use another friend.

"Okay." She sighed, hooking her pinky with Evie's, who let out a squeal of delight. "One date and that's it."

"I promise. Declan Owen will rock your world."

Declan Owen pulled into the parking lot of his apartment building and sighed. He was dogshit tired from a long day's work. Shutting off his truck, he glanced around the lot. His neighbor's car was parked not too far from his. He had been trying to avoid her at all costs the last few weeks. Apparently she had decided he needed a woman in his life and she'd be the perfect person to match him up.

Declan Owen didn't need help finding a woman. He had plenty that he could call on if he were to ever get lonely.

He stepped out of his truck and grabbed his duffle bag from the back seat. It had been a long day for the SWAT sergeant. His team had been called out to two incidents, and he was beat. He just wanted to take a shower, drink a cold beer or two, and then crash on either his couch or his bed. He wasn't picky.

Dec entered his complex and quickly checked his mailbox. It was a small building, three stories tall, and housed two apartments on each level. Grabbing the few bits of mail he had in his box, he made his way up to the second floor where his apartment was located.

He tried to get inside his home before his nosey neighbor heard him, but he was too late.

"Dec!" Evie's cheerful voice called out from behind him.

He blew out a deep breath and turned.

"Hey, Evie," he murmured, trying to keep all emotions from his face. No matter how many times he scowled at her, growled, or just put on his best 'fuck off' attitude, she seemed to see right through him. Her bubbly personality just couldn't take a hint.

"Long day at work? You look beat," she said, leaning against her doorjamb. She was sporting two blonde pigtails on top of her head.

If he hadn't known her age, he would have assumed she was about twelve. A background check he had run on her when she'd moved in confirmed she was twenty-seven.

"Yeah, long day. Have a good night." He nodded to her and turned his back, hefting his duffle bag on his shoulder. He stepped over the threshold into his apartment and paused as he felt a presence behind him.

"You remember my friend from work I was telling you about?" Evie asked, standing in his doorway.

He sighed and sent up a prayer that his nosey little

neighbor would get the hint that he just wanted to be alone.

"Evie, I'm dead on my feet—"

"This won't take long. So I asked my friend again, and she said yes!" A wide grin broke out on her face, and she hopped in one place.

"Evie, I've told you a million times—"

"Aw, come on, Dec. Who better to show the new girl a good time than you?"

"But, Evie—"

"You're a cop, so I know she would be safe. I wouldn't want to hook her up with just anyone. Please?" Her wide eyes pleaded with him, and she crossed her fingers.

He glanced up at the ceiling of his dark apartment and sent up a prayer that he wouldn't regret this decision.

"Okay, Evie. One date."

He cringed at her squeal of joy.

"Thank you so much, Dec. You won't regret it at all. You and Aspen will go great together."

He watched her skip back to her apartment and shut the door. He stood frozen, unsure of when he had lost control of his dating life.

2

Declan was a man of his word. He agreed to go on the date with Evie's friend and, dammit, he'd do it. After this favor, he'd have a sit-down with his neighbor to discuss boundaries.

He made a reservation at a local restaurant that would be perfect for a first date. It had a nice bar and great food. He'd been there a few times but usually went for happy hour after a long shift.

He glanced down at the clock on the dash of his truck—he was going to arrive early. He couldn't even remember the last time he'd been on a blind date. He snorted. Come to think of it, he'd never been on a blind date before.

Declan Owen never needed to be hooked up. He knew that he drew in females without even trying. His physique and his looks were all that he'd ever needed. He wasn't in need of a girlfriend. Men like him didn't do well in relationships.

Dating a cop was hard.

Dating a SWAT officer was almost unbearable.

He'd do this favor this one night. Be good company to Aspen Hale, and then they'd part ways, never seeing each other again. After dinner, he'd probably reach out to one of his regular women he called when he had an itch that needed scratching.

Bachelor for life.

He'd thought his best friend would have been the same, but Marcas MacArthur had found a woman worth giving his name to. Mac and Sarena were perfect together. Declan already loved Sarena like a sister and couldn't wait for the two to tie the knot. As the best man, it was his job to ensure Mac made it to the altar.

Declan's thoughts trailed back to a few months ago when that all could have changed. Sarena had been kidnapped by a gang who was trying to retaliate against Mac. The leader of the gang, Silas Tyree, had orches- trated a plot to get revenge on Mac for killing his cousin, and Sarena just so happened to be object of the gangster's revenge.

That night, Declan hadn't hesitated on killing the gangster. Mac had given himself up for the safety of Sarena, and Declan had refused to let his friend down. The minute he'd had a clear shot, he'd put a bullet in the middle of the gangster's forehead, saving his friend.

Mac would have done the same for him.

It was an unspoken word between the two of them. They had served in the Navy together and now worked SWAT together. They were brothers for life.

The minute Mac had informed him that he cared for Sarena and she meant something to him, Declan knew he'd protect her with his life just as Mac would.

The shooting of the gangster had led to a paid leave for Declan. It had been investigated, and he was cleared. The killing of the gangster was deemed justified.

But they still had one problem.

There was a leak in the department.

Someone had told the gangster it was Mac who'd put down his cousin. They still had yet to discover who the rat was.

Not knowing if sensitive information was hitting the streets made what they did more dangerous. The discovery of the leak led IRB to get in everyone's ass at the station. There was still no word on who it was.

But that didn't mean Declan couldn't investigate it without anyone knowing. Because of the leak, his friend suffered. That twenty-four-hour period when Sarena had first gone missing had been hell on Mac. In all the years he'd known Mac, Declan had never seen him lose it before. The tortured look in Mac's eyes was something Declan prayed he would not ever have to experience himself.

Declan put on his blinker and coasted his truck to a stop in front of the restaurant. He patiently waited for the oncoming traffic to pay before turning into the parking lot of the restaurant. He found a decent spot and shut the truck off.

He glanced over at the building and blew out a deep breath. According to Evie, Aspen would be wearing a black dress and would have a flower in her long black hair.

Entering the establishment, he was greeted by the hostess. Her gaze perused his body, and a wide smile spread across her face. He'd seen the look plenty of times. She was easy on the eyes, but just not his type.

He'd kept his attire to semi-dress. A black button-down shirt and slacks.

"Welcome to Donnie's. How may I help you?" she greeted him as he arrived in front of her.

He glanced down at her name tag with Julie written across it.

"Hello, Julie." He smiled and easily read the interest in her eyes. He shrugged. Maybe after dinner with Aspen, he would take Julie up on her unspoken offer. It wouldn't do any harm. He'd keep his promise to Evie and then would be free to do as he pleased. He informed Julie that he was meeting someone.

"The other half of your party is already at the bar. I

can show you the way," she offered, gesturing towards the bar.

"No need. I know where it is." He shook his head, moved past her, and headed down the short hall that led to the bar.

"Um, Mr. Owen," Julie called out behind him.

He turned to find her smiling.

She tucked her dark hair behind her ear. "If it doesn't work out with your friend, I get off in an hour."

He threw her a wink and a smile. "Duly noted."

He continued on and chuckled. Maybe this night would be lucky. He entered the bar area and scanned the counter, zeroing in on the only person at the bar that could be Aspen.

His breath caught in his throat as he took her in from afar. Even in the low-light establishment, he could see her beauty from where he stood. Her bronze skin practically glowed. Her long hair flowed down her back in curls. A flower was tucked in behind her ear, holding her hair back. She stood at the bar sipping on a drink. Her black dress did nothing to hide her curvy frame.

Declan's mouth watered at the sight of her body. Another man coming to stand next to her brought on a growl that escaped from his chest. Before he realized it, his feet were already carrying him across the room.

"Hey, pretty lady. A man shouldn't let someone as beautiful as you wait," the man was saying.

Declan casually made his way to Aspen's other side.

"Let me buy you a drink," the stranger pressed.

"No, thank you," she replied casually, barely looking at the man.

Declan almost felt sorry for the guy, who was average-looking and hitting on her. Declan wasn't sure why, but he was itching to plow his fist directly in the jerk's face.

"Your date is —"

"Right here," Declan growled, sending a glare the man's way. He knew that better men couldn't return his glare, and this one just shrank back, his gaze meeting Declan's.

Aspen turned toward him, and their eyes connected. Lust and need slammed into his chest as he gazed into her dark irises. His attention traveled down toward her plump lips that he wanted to slam his mouth to, but he figured he'd at least introduce himself first. His perusal trailed farther, and he had to fight to adjust his cock that was pressing against his pants. Her dress dipped low to put her ample breasts on display.

"Are you sure—" the man stuttered, but Declan flickered his eyes back to him, cutting him off.

If he didn't get the message, Declan was sure his fist would deliver it more clearly.

He got the message.

He visibly swallowed and nodded before walking away.

"Declan, I presume?" She leaned against the counter. Her perfectly sculpted eyebrow rose as she studied him. Her gaze made its own way down his body.

He had to control his breathing.

He wanted her.

Maybe he owed Evie a thank you.

"Yes, ma'am," he murmured, leaning closer to her.

She tilted her head back and studied him some more. He returned the favor and could see that she was guarded.

Alarms went off in the back of his head, but he pushed them back. This was a blind date, of course she'd be guarded.

"Well, Evie certainly did not fib. You are quite handsome," she said, a small smile appearing on her lips.

"I'd have to say that she fibbed to me." He had to touch her. He reached up and readjusted her flower that didn't need to be adjusted. He just needed to find a way to get a hand on her. He trailed his fingers down the side of her face, caressing her soft brown skin.

"She did?" Her sexy little eyebrow rose again.

"Yes, she didn't tell me how sexy and beautiful you were," he said.

Her smile widened at his words.

Pleased that she seemed to relax with him, he held out his arm. "Shall we?"

"We shall."

3

I'm a lady. I'm a fucking lady, Aspen had to chant to herself. *I will not throw myself at this man.*

Declan Owen was all man, and his heated gazes had her taking another healthy sip of her wine. Her eyes met his across the table, and she bit her lip to keep from moaning aloud.

When he'd first arrived at her side and saved her from the third man trying to hit on her, she had thought she had died and gone to Heaven. She couldn't take her eyes off him. His hard glare had sent the nameless guy scrambling away. It was definitely a turn on for her.

His alpha personality weakened her legs. There was nothing sexier than a man who was in control and knew how to exert himself. Her breath had been ripped from her lungs the moment he'd turned his attention to her. His eyes had practically undressed her, leaving her body strung tight.

Their dinner had been going well. She tried to avoid certain questions as she had been instructed. She had to remember everything she had been coached since entering the witness protection program. She couldn't go into too much information about herself. He, on the other hand, was open about growing up in Charleston, South Carolina, serving in the Navy and working SWAT now. He seemed to be an all-round great guy.

She bit back a sigh.

Again, her life was taken from her and was being guided in a direction she had no control over. Nothing would be able to come from this date.

Declan was great with his conversation and would be the type of guy she'd pursue, but alas, her future was still blank. Soon, she'd have to go back to California and testify against the man who was like an uncle to her, who she'd gone to confront about her findings and witnessed him kill someone in front of her.

She tried to push away the memory of the faceless man's body hitting the floor before her.

"I guess I'm losing my touch," Declan's voice broke through her thoughts.

"I'm sorry." She tried to smile and met his eyes. But her attempt at smiling was lost on him. He read right through her.

"I seem to have lost you for a second. Is everything

all right?" He cocked his head to the side, his curious eyes studying her.

The sound of music filled the air. She looked over at the band that began playing. She smiled, taking in a few couples making their way to the dance floor.

What she wouldn't give to just have a normal life. One where she didn't have to worry that someone would try to kill her to keep her from spilling secrets.

"Yes, everything's fine," she lied. She wiped her mouth with her napkin and knew that he knew she was lying. She swiveled her eyes back to the couples dancing to the music. The sound of Declan's chair pushing back from the table grabbed her attention. She watched as he made his way around their table.

She greedily took him in. The man was physically fit, and it was apparent that he took care of himself. He'd folded his sleeves, displaying his tattooed forearms. Aspen wasn't sure when she began thinking forearms were sexy, but his definitely did something for her.

"Dance with me," he murmured, holding his hand out.

Without hesitation, she placed her smaller one in his and allowed him to pull her from the chair. She may not know what the future held for her, but she was willing to grab on to what she could for the moment, and if dinner and dancing with Declan was right now, she'd take it.

He guided her to the dance floor and swung her around before pulling her close to him. She gasped as her body molded against his. He left no room in between them. His hard length pushed into her stomach. She bit her lip and tilted her head back to gaze up into his hooded eyes. Their bodies fit together perfectly. Everywhere he was hard, she was soft. She felt protected in his arms while their bodies swayed to the music. Declan knew exactly what he was doing. He was wooing her.

She wouldn't be able to resist the temptation of Declan Owen. She'd tossed caution to the wind. She'd take this night and hold on to it. She'd be selfish and take great pleasure with Declan. Tomorrow, she'd go back to her everyday routine that she'd established here in Columbia.

"So do all you southern boys know how to dance?" she murmured, loving the feel of his hand on the small of her back. For someone who was as large as he was, Declan sure knew how to move. Dancing was one of her favorite pastimes, and tonight she had a great partner.

"My mother believed all southern boys should learn the basics." He laughed, twirling her around before bringing her flush to his body again.

"Well, one day, I'll have to thank Mrs. Owen for teaching her son how to dance." She laughed, too, but then caught what she'd said. She held back a curse at her slip-up.

There would be no future meeting of families.

He must have felt her stiffen. A frown appeared on his face before disappearing. She avoided his eyes and laid her head on his strong chest, her thoughts racing. She closed her eyes and tried to relax, but Declan's hand on the small of her back slid down lower onto the swell of her ass.

The sexual tension surrounding them could be cut with a knife. His body called to hers, and it was getting harder to resist. It didn't help that he wasn't even hiding his hard length from her.

"So, Sergeant Owen, is that a gun in your pants, or are you just happy to be dancing with me?" she asked, trying not to laugh at her horrible attempt at a joke.

"Oh, I'm very happy to be dancing with you," he growled, his fingers digging into the meat of her ass.

She bit her lip again and eased back to glance up at him. His hooded eyes met hers. She slid her hand up his hard chest, and it found its way to the nape of his neck. He slowly lowered his head to hers and covered her lips with his.

She sighed and leaned into him. His tongue thrust forth, sweeping into her mouth to meet hers. She wasn't shy in meeting his tongue with hers. The kiss was downright scathing hot, open and deep. The restaurant was forgotten; she was lost in Declan's kiss. Her nipples painfully pushed against her bra, demanding to be set free.

The attraction between them was intense and had Aspen wanting to climb up and wrap her legs around Declan, but the dance floor was certainly not the place. A small protest escaped her lips, and he pulled back and leaned his forehead on hers. They both were slightly out of breath from the kiss. Aspen's body was on fire for him. She entwined her fingers at the base of his neck.

"Wow," she gasped.

"Aspen, I don't want to lead you on or anything," he said.

Her eyes flew open.

Doubt entered her mind. Was the attraction all one-sided? Did he not feel what she felt?

"Okay," she responded slowly, unsure of where he was going with this.

"I don't do relationships," he began.

She bit back a sigh of relief. As much as she would want to see where this thing with him would go, she couldn't afford to be in a relationship. She had too much on her plate at the moment.

"I know you feel what is between us," he said.

She nodded, their bodies slowly swaying with the beat of the music. The feel of his hands on her made it hard for her to concentrate. His possessive touch was obvious every time she glanced around and saw another man eyeing her. Declan would shoot off a glare to warn them off.

"I want you," he declared.

The muscles of her stomach quivered at the hunger in his eyes. Relief filled her. She gripped him tight to her, pushing her breasts against his chest.

His nostrils flared as she smiled up at him. "I don't want to lie or make any excuses at all.

"I want you, too," she replied. She shyly lowered her eyes to his stubble. The dark shadow on his chin had her fingers itching to rub his jaw. She ached to feel the stubble between her thighs. She traced her hand down his chest and settled it over his heart, unsure how to make the offer for him to come back to her apartment.

"No strings is what I'm offering."

Their bodies paused. He stared down at her while she contemplated his admission. Little did he realize that 'no strings' was right up her alley.

Sex.

That's what he was putting on the table. With the state of her life right now, that's all she wanted.

No strings.

Just someone who could work her body into a delicious orgasm.

She knew Declan could be that man.

"Will you come home with me?" she asked, raising her eyebrow. He'd put the offer on the table, and she was accepting.

Graciously.

The growl that vibrated from his chest had her core clenching.

"Let's get out of here."

4

Declan drove them to Aspen's home. He didn't like the thought of her walking to the restaurant. Her home was only a few minutes' car drive away. He kept flicking his eyes to Aspen while she sat quiet in the passenger seat.

"Two more houses and that's me on the left. The one with the light on. Just pull up to the side door." She pointed at a cozy little home.

He nodded and followed her directions. He knew the area and wasn't sure he liked her living in this part of town. He parked in her driveway between the two houses and turned to her, finding her eyes already on him. It was late, and the street was dark and deserted.

"Are you sure about this?" he asked. He knew they had only just met, but he needed to be certain that she was on board with what he was asking. Something was off about her. He couldn't put his finger on what it was.

Every time she mentioned something about the future, she almost shut down.

"Yeah, I'm sure." She nodded with a small smile lingering on her lips.

He dropped his gaze to her plump lips and ached to taste them again. He reached for her, and she came willingly. He gripped her by the neck, crushing his lips to hers.

Her mouth opened immediately. The kiss was hard and desperate. He thrust his tongue inside her mouth, meeting hers. Her groan fueled his desire for her. She climbed over the arm console and straddled him.

Her fingers dove in his hair, and he angled his head to deepen the kiss. He gripped her ass tight, bringing her core flush with his cock that was straining to burst out of his slacks.

She released a moan as he trailed a string of kisses along her jawline and toward her neck. The smell of her scent filled his nostrils. He breathed in deeply, memorizing the sweet smell of her perfume and her womanly scent.

"Declan," she groaned.

He slid his hand beneath the edge of her dress, moving it along her supple thighs and disappearing farther, exploring her soft skin. He found her panties and pushed them to the side and dipped his finger between her slick labia.

"Yes."

He locked his eyes on her as she gripped the back of his neck. She took his breath away with all the emotions flashing across her face. He found her swollen clitoris with his finger.

"Aspen, baby," he muttered, unable to take his eyes off her.

She rode his fingers, threw her head back, thrusting her breasts toward him, and he was lost to her. He knew they should move this into the house. Taking her for the first time in his truck wasn't how he'd imagined their first time together, but at the moment, there was no way he could stop.

They were sliding down a hill at full speed with no brakes.

Unable to resist, he reached with his free hand and pulled the top of her dress down, revealing her breasts. Her hips thrust against his hand as he continued to stroke her clit. He quickly undid the clasp of her bra, freeing her beautiful mounds.

"Fuck me," he ordered, taking the first one in his mouth. He gripped it with his hand, bathing her taut nipple with his tongue before suckling it deep within his mouth.

Her gasps and moans filled the air.

"Declan."

His name on her tongue had him harder than steel.

"Aspen, take me out of my pants," he urged, releasing her breast from his lips.

Her eyes flickered to his, and she reached down between them. His cock pressed painfully against his shorts underneath his pants while she struggled with the belt and button.

"I have to warn you, it's been a while," she said, finally opening his pants.

"Don't worry, I'll take care of you," he promised.

She slid her hand inside of his boxer briefs.

Sweat beaded on his forehead. Her hand encircled this thick length. He bit back a curse as she worked to free him from his pants. He couldn't even remember the last time he'd had sex in a vehicle. They were both acting like horny teenagers and both laughed and shifted, trying to make sex work in his truck.

He reached down and adjusted the seat, giving them more room.

"Sorry, pretty lady. I haven't done this since I was a teenager." He chuckled.

"You haven't had sex since you were a teen—"

"No...yes, I've had sex since I was a teenager," he stammered. He laughed at her wide-eyed look. Plenty of sex. At the moment, she had him just as flustered as a boy with his first girl. He didn't know what it was about her, but all of his blood had headed south, leaving his brain to fumble for responses. He needed to hurry and bury his cock deep in her. The feel of her slowly stroking his length was making it harder to think. "I just meant in a car."

"Oh." She bit her lip. A sheepish expression fell across her face. "Well, I thought you were going to say you were a born again virgin or something. I wouldn't want to take advantage of you."

"Come here." He pulled her close with a growl, the tip of his cock brushing her slick folds. He couldn't wait any longer. He lined up the blunt tip of his cock with her slit and guided her down onto him.

The sound of her deep moan tore through the air as she impaled herself on his length. He thrust forward, fully seating himself in her tight sheath. Tiny beads of sweat slid down his temples, and he tried to concentrate on not blowing his load.

He released a curse at the tightness of Aspen's walls. She was a small woman, and he was fighting the urge to pound into her.

"Oh God," she cried out.

"I got to move." He lifted her and slammed her back down.

Aspen's fingers dug into his shoulders, and she moved along with the pace he set. He locked his gaze on her face. Her eyes were squeezed shut with pure pleasure plastered on her face.

He dug his fingers in to her ass and guided her up and down on his length.

"Declan," she gasped.

Her breasts danced in front of his face. His tongue ached to taste her again. He pulled her forward to allow him to capture her bobbing breast in his mouth. Her fingers threaded their way into his hair, gripping him to her as she rode him hard.

The sounds of their coupling filled the air while the heat of their passion steamed up the windows. They were lost in their own little world. The familiar feeling of his release built in his testicles.

"Aspen," he ground out, increasing their pace. He didn't want to release before her. He wanted them to go together. "Come with me."

Her eyes flashed open and locked with his. He let go of her breast and eased her face down and crushed his mouth to hers, capturing her scream. Her body shuddered with her hitting the peak. Her pussy walls clamped down on him, and his orgasm slammed into him. He tore his lips from her mouth and roared, shooting his seed deep within her womb.

In bed, Aspen sighed and buried her face into Declan's

warm chest. She slowly drifted her hand across his hard abdomen. She was lost in the memories of their night together. The sun was now coming up, and she didn't want their time to come to an end, but unfortunately, it was. He'd wake up, they would have awkward conversation while they got dressed, and then he would leave.

This was what she wanted.

A night full of passion that would last her for a while.

His gentle snores filled the air, and she contemplated how she would wake him. She had a few ideas but knew she shouldn't act on them since he had to leave.

She hated to wake him, but it was time. It was time for her to break the perfect night that they'd had. She didn't want to have the awkward morning after. She'd act cool and collected while he gathered his things and left.

She just couldn't guarantee she wouldn't bawl her eyes out after he'd gone.

She wouldn't cry because he was leaving, but because of how her life had come to be.

Lonely.

Aspen pulled back and sat up, taking in Declan's perfect muscular chest, his washboard abs with the light sprinkle of dark hair that continued south of the blankets.

She bit her lip and had to tear her gaze away from his sublime body. Her heart raced at memories of her tongue burning a trail down his abdomen and ending with his cock in her mouth. The taste of him still lingered.

Pushing those memories aside, she slid from the bed and quietly made her way over to her closet and grabbed her robe. This was new for her, and she wasn't sure how to end a one-night stand, but there was no time like the present to learn. She walked over to Declan who was stirring.

"Hey." She gently tapped his shoulder.

His eyes flew open, clouded with sleep at first before focusing on her. His lips curved up in a smile as he ran his hand through his hair, leaving it tousled.

"Morning," he murmured, sitting against the headboard.

"It's almost eight o'clock," she whispered.

His smile slowly disappeared when the reason she'd woke him settled in.

It was time for him to go.

She hated how he appeared to shut down right in front of her. Their night together had been amazing, and it was a shame she couldn't afford to see where this thing between them could go.

But then again, all he was offering was no strings attached.

"Yeah, thanks for waking me." He swung his feet to the floor.

"No problem." She took a few steps away from him before she jumped back into the bed with him. She turned on her heel and rushed out the room. She didn't want to give in and ask him to stay with her for breakfast.

They had made an agreement.

No strings.

She arrived in her kitchen and immediately went straight for the coffee maker with her mind racing.

One-night stands didn't stay for breakfast, did they?

5

Declan pulled his ballistics vest over his head as his team prepared to go out on a call. He was lost in his thoughts, still confused on the situation with Aspen. He should have been grateful there wasn't any drama.

He'd gotten what he wanted.

A night with no strings.

But it still left him baffled.

He was at first pleased to find her standing next to him when he had awakened. Her beautiful bronze skin had practically glowed against her silk white robe. In the hours of the night, he had tasted every single facet of her body. He would have preferred to have woken up with her still tucked into his side.

'It's almost eight o'clock.'

Her words still echoed in his head. The mention of the time had been like a splash of cold water to the face.

He had been dismissed.

She hadn't been cold, but she hadn't asked for his number or to even see him again. Declan was used to being in the role of having to let women down and even reminding them that it was to be for only one night.

Aspen had just sent him on his way with an awesome cup of coffee in a to-go cup, and a smile.

"Sergeant Owen."

Mac's sharp voice broke through his thoughts. Shutting his locker, he turned and faced his longtime friend.

Marcas MacArthur's attention was locked on Declan. Mac was like a bulldog—once he got something or someone in his sights, he didn't let it rest until he got what he wanted.

The locker room drew quiet as Mac made his way to him. His teammates were not hiding the fact that they wanted to hear the conversation between him and Mac.

"What's going on, Dec? You're barely here," Mac said, stopping in front of him.

"Just not feeling well today, Mac." He met his friend's eyes. There was no way he would admit to being hung up on a one-night stand. Today was just not the day to get his balls busted over a woman.

"Why don't you sit this one out. Head home and get some rest. You look like shit."

"I'm good." He straightened to his full height and met the stares of his teammates.

He would be good for the assignment. His men would depend on him being sharp once they got to the location.

Apparently satisfied, Mac walked away and began briefing them on the job.

"We have a hostage situation down at the Comet's main terminal hub. Our local boys in blue were able to secure the perimeter and need our help extracting the hostages and grabbing the bad guys."

"Any reason given?" Ashton, the SWAT team's lead negotiator asked.

"Sounds like the transit heads were laying off some of the bus drivers, and they weren't taking kind to it," Mac replied. "Let's roll out. I'll give more information in the B.E.A.R."

The team filed out and headed toward their armored vehicle, all dressed in their black fatigues with SWAT brandished across the front of their ballistics vests. Declan could still feel eyes on him and knew that Mac didn't fully believe him. His friend knew when we was lying.

Declan tried to act busy, double-checking his weapons and securing his helmet on his head. They all wore face masks that covered the bottom of their faces to protect their identity when it came to high-risk situations.

Zain Roman, a longtime member of the team, hopped in the driver's seat while the rest filed in the back.

Myles Burton, the team's sniper, sat across from Declan and eyed him. He nodded to his team mate who seemed to be checking him out as Mac had.

They were a close-knit unit and would sense when someone was off.

"You good?" Myles asked, cocking an eyebrow.

"I'm good."

"All right, men, intelligence states that the bad guys have ten Comet employees housed in the dispatch room of the bus terminal." Mac continued the briefing, but Declan didn't hear a word that was spoken.

His thoughts were on Aspen. The memory of her creamy brown skin sliding against his had his cock jerking. He tried to shake off the memories, but they kept flooding his brain.

Her gasps when he'd thrust deep within her had him rubbing a hand along his face. He cringed when he hit the rough bristles of his jawline. He hadn't shaved in a few days and was paying for it.

He hadn't felt like this for a woman in...damn, he couldn't even remember.

They arrived at the local city bus station where all

hell had broken loose. The team instantly jumped from the B.E.A.R and sprang into action. The terminal was a large building that usually bustled with guests and employees, but today, it was a ghost town.

Ashton and Mac went to speak with the lead investigator on the scene. Ashton would be the one assisting with the negotiations of the hostages. Declan and the others spread out, speaking with the cops that were the first on the scene and ensuring that the perimeter was pushed back. The men in the terminal were armed and pissed off. There was no telling how they would react, and they had to ensure the safety of the public.

"We have blueprints," Brodie said, gathering the team over to the hood of a squad car.

They all stood around and began planning the entry into the terminal.

Their team was specially trained to respond to certain situations. The local boys in blue depended on Declan and the rest of the SWAT team to infiltrate and secure all targets, preventing loss of life.

They had intensive training that made them all experts on infiltrating. Their training was drilled into them so much that Declan was sure his team mates could practically do their job blindfolded.

Confident they had a well-thought-out plan, the team moved and waited for the order.

"They're sending out three women," Ashton called out.

Declan, Brodie, Zain, and Iker moved in formation toward the building. They would escort the hostages to safety. A few ambulances were parked back behind the yellow tape, to offer assessment of the hostages and check for injuries.

Their weapons were aimed high as they stood near the doorway of the large terminal. They flanked the glass sliding doors and waited for the women to come forth.

"I see them." Brodie knelt on the ground beside Declan.

"How many?" he asked.

"Looks like the three as promised," Brodie said.

The three women ran out of the building with tears running down their faces. Declan and his men surrounded them, putting their bodies in the line of fire as they rushed them to safety. Uniformed officers met them and escorted the women over to the ambulance.

"Have they made any demands?" Declan asked, walking over to where Mac and Ashton stood.

"Yes, they want to speak to the CEO of Comet. They're demanding their jobs back," Ashton said. "Not sure if that will happen. Give me more time."

"Take your time." Mac slapped him on the back.

"We need to get the hostages out safely. Let's not have any casualties today."

Aspen made her way to the break room for her lunch. She pushed open the door to find the place empty, but the television was turned to the local news station that was streaming a breaking story.

Everyone in the library was talking about the hostage situation down at the Comet's main terminal. It had been going on for hours, and the local SWAT team had been dispatched.

Her thoughts turned to Declan. She knew he was one of the SWAT officers, and her heart sped up that he may be in danger. She sighed and sat at the table. It wasn't for her to worry about the sexy cop. They'd had their one night together with no strings attached.

"Please tell me you have it on the news," Evie gasped, blowing into the break room.

"Yup," Aspen replied, opening her packed lunch. She took a bite of her sandwich with her gaze glued to the table. Not much happened in the city, but when it did, the press was all over the story.

"Declan is probably there right in the middle of this craziness," Evie said, plopping down next to Aspen.

They both ate their food in silence for a while as the anchors were giving updates on the situation.

"I just hope everyone is okay." Aspen took in the chaos taking place not too far from the library.

"So, what happened with you and Declan?" Evie asked, turning to Aspen.

The television went to commercials.

Aspen had been dreading this conversation. There was no way she was telling Evie she had slept with Declan. If she did that, Evie would be practically planning their wedding.

"Nothing. He seems like a nice guy." She took a sip of her water as an excuse stop talking.

"And..." Evie's wide eyes were on her.

"Well, we met at the restaurant. Had dinner, and that was it." She shrugged as if it were no big deal. She refused to look her friend in the eyes for fear that Evie would see the truth in hers. She was always a shitty liar.

"That's it? No spark, no instant romance, no hot sex all night?"

Aspen coughed at Evie's line of questioning. She almost choked on her sandwich but took her time swallowing the food. Oh, there had been plenty of sparks and hot sex. Just thinking of the things they had done had her body heating up at the moment. She grabbed her water bottle and swallowed a healthy sip. She didn't want to give away any hint on how just thinking of Declan Owen had her getting all hot and bothered.

She shook her head, turning her attention back to the television as the commercials ended.

"No, Evie. I'm sorry."

"Well, damn. I must be losing my touch. I was so sure you two would be perfect for each other." Evie sighed.

"It looks as if the SWAT team has been successful in today's intense hostage situation. We are getting reports that all the hostages are unharmed," the anchor woman on the television announced. The camera switched back to the scene and zeroed in on two men in all back with face masks on, bringing two men in handcuffs out of the bus terminal.

She focused on one of the men. She knew that body and the walk.

Intimately.

Declan decked out in his uniform had her heart racing. She never knew seeing a man with his tactical gear could be so sexy.

Dirty thoughts entered her mind that involved him, his ballistics vest, and handcuffs.

She sighed and pushed those thoughts aside for now.

But it didn't mean she couldn't fantasize about him in the privacy of her own home.

Her cell buzzed in her pocket. She grabbed her phone and pulled it out and swiped the glass screen. She gripped it tight as she read a message from US Marshall Ball. He wanted to move up their meeting.

Apprehension filled her, and her mind raced. He'd never moved up their appointments before. She responded and confirmed that she could meet him at the new time.

"Everything okay?" Evie's voice broke through her thoughts.

She looked at her friend and nodded.

She hoped it was.

6

His music blared from the speakers in his truck as he drove toward downtown. Declan had a meeting in city hall that he couldn't miss. He had a private appointment with one of the IRB agents. He couldn't let a leak in their department go unanswered. That leak could have cost them Mac's life.

After the bus terminal situation, Mac had chewed him out. Declan had been distracted by a brown-skinned beauty, and this distraction could have cost *him* his life.

The startled targets had shot off a round of bullets, and one had embedded in the wall next to Declan's head.

It would have been a fatal shot.

He was starting to rethink this no-strings clause he had proposed to Aspen. He hadn't been able to get her out of his mind. Apparently, Aspen had no issues with sending him on his way.

It bothered him.

It couldn't have been the sex. There was no way she was that good of an actress. Every orgasm she'd had was genuine.

And here he was, not knowing if he should contact her.

For the first time ever, he was thinking of pursuing something with a woman, and it scared him. He knew better than to try to speak with Mac. Mac, who was currently engaged to be married, wouldn't be the best person to ask. He was far too in love with Sarena. Any advice he'd offer would be clouded with his feelings for Sarena.

Declan was thinking of maybe starting a physical-only type of relationship with Aspen. He didn't have her number but knew where she lived.

Yeah, he'd be labeled as a stalker if he just showed up. He racked his brain and knew Evie would have her number. He shuddered with the thought of showing interest in Aspen to her. She'd never let him live it down.

He didn't have many choices.

Maybe he'd call his sister, Averi. She was the only one he could trust who would give sound advice regarding his situation and not judge him. They had a close relationship, and he knew that would be the best thing to do.

He turned on the street leading to City Hall, and a familiar figure walking down the street caught his eye.

Aspen.

He took in her beautiful silhouette, and his heart pounded. He quickly found a parking spot on the street and rushed from his truck. He slammed the door and tried to remain cool.

"Aspen!" he called.

She paused and turned to him with a surprised look on her face.

He jogged toward her.

He was not stalking her.

This was just a coincidence.

"Hello, Declan." She smiled as he reached her side.

He was captivated by her bright smile and stood before her, unsure what to say.

Did they hug? Shake hands? He wasn't sure so just kept his hands to himself and greedily took her in.

"How are you?" he asked.

Her guarded look unsettled him, plus that her smile didn't quite reach her eyes. Those alarms in the back of his mind were going off

He thought hard and didn't recognize this feeling in his chest.

Was this nervousness?

"I'm good," she said.

They fell in step with each other down the sidewalk. He tried not to stare at her. Her dark hair was left flowing down her bare back, thanks to her summer dress. His hands ached to touch her, but he had to fight the inclination.

"Where are you off to?" he asked, curious to know where she would be going at this time of day. It was early in the morning to just be walking downtown.

"Just some personal business at City Hall." She shrugged her bronze shoulders. "Where are you headed?"

"Same. I have some police business in the mayor's office," he murmured.

The continued in a comfortable silence and arrived at the main door of the building. He opened the door for her and caught a whiff of her perfume and had to hold back a growl. He entered behind her and couldn't keep his gaze from dropping down to the swell of her ass.

His cock hardened at the sight, and he knew he couldn't let her leave without him getting her number or another date.

The foyer had a grand staircase that led up to the second level where offices were located.

"See you around, Declan." She smiled softly and walked toward the staircase.

He jumped into action and grabbed her arm. "Go out with me again," he blurted out.

Smooth, man, real smooth.

Her eyes widened as she glanced up at him. He gently caressed her skin and refused to let go of her arm. He glanced down at their connection and loved seeing his lighter skin against her caramel. It was one of the biggest turn ons for him.

He stepped closer to her, and she looked away from him. The bustle of people moving around the first level ignored them. At the moment, he didn't care who was watching. He needed an answer from her.

"Please." He moved his fingers down her arm and entwined them with hers. "A lunch date or dinner again. Your choice."

She studied his eyes, and he waited for her to make her decision.

"But I thought it was to be no strings?"

"Do we ever know what we really want?" He locked his gaze on her.

She seemed to be mulling it over.

He needed her to say yes. "It's just a date."

"Yes," she said with a smile to her lips. She backed away from him, breaking their connection. "I have to go or I'll be late for my appointment."

"I need your telephone number," he announced. For their date, Evie had set up the entire thing, so he hadn't spoken to Aspen before they'd met. "I don't think we will be needing Evie to set this one up."

She chuckled as she came back to him. They exchanged numbers, and he couldn't keep the smile from his face. She turned away with a wave. He watched her walk up the stairs until she couldn't see her any longer. He turned and strode down the grand hallway to go have his meeting at the mayor's office.

A strong sense of déjà vu was settling over Aspen as she sat in the chair across from US Marshal Ball.

"What are you saying?" she asked, unsure of what he was explaining to her.

He took his glasses off, rested them on the table, and stared at her. She bit her lip, apprehension filling her chest. She wanted all of this over with so she could make something out of the life she'd been given. It wasn't what it was, and according to the man sitting across from her, it wouldn't ever be.

"The timeline for you to be back in California has moved up. You will be needed to testify earlier than expected."

"What?" she exclaimed, sitting forward in her chair. She was floored. There was no way she was ready to face him in court. She turned toward the window and took in the beautiful blue sky, the memories of that night surfacing.

Her heels echoed on the marble floors as she made her way toward the executive offices. She braced her evidence against her chest. She was still in disbelief at what she had uncovered.

Her father had been right.

Someone was embezzling money from the company, and it was in the millions.

That someone was none other than her father's best friend and partner, Ray Acosta. He was like an uncle to her. She'd known him her entire life. He had been with her father since he'd created the company. Her father had brought him in a few years later once the company had got off the ground. He was one of her father's most trusted associates.

And he had betrayed him.

As a forensic accountant, this was her specialty. Had she not been a specialist, then she may not have caught the disappearance of the money. Someone had been paying contracts to dummy corporations, and she had figured it out. She had yet to contact her father and wanted to confront Ray herself.

It was late in the evening, and the offices were empty, but she was sure he was still in his. She needed to hear why he was stealing from the company before turning all of her evidence over to the authorities in the morning. If he were in trouble, her father would have helped him.

Raised voices traveled down the hallway, and she slowed. Who would be here this late arguing? Her footsteps faltered, then she continued on toward Ray's office. The voices grew louder once she arrived at his door that was left ajar.

Ray sat behind his desk with a man sitting in the chair in front. Two large men stood behind Ray, shouting at each other.

"I don't care," Ray snapped.

"You are getting sloppy," the man in the chair growled. "I can't keep covering for you anymore."

"You aren't going to do a damn thing but what you've been doing." Ray leaned back in his chair.

Her breath caught in her throat. She knew she should move away from the door, but she was captivated on what was going on before her.

"Ray. I'm done. You don't pay me enough to take your bullshit." The man stood suddenly, almost knocking the chair over.

"You don't have a choice." Ray's voice dropped low.

Aspen leaned closer to the door and stifled a gasp. Ray held a gun on the man while the two goons behind him moved forward.

"What are you doing?" the man asked. "You don't have the fucking balls to pull that trigger. I've been doing all your dirty work."

"Now see, that's where you're wrong. I choose when

to get my hands dirty." Ray stood, and she watched in horror as he pulled the trigger.

The sounds of gunfire filled the air. Aspen held her breath. The man's body jerked a few times, then he stumbled back, falling over his chair and landing on the floor.

"No," she cried out.

Eyes turned to her. She shook her head and backed away from the door.

"Aspen!" Ray hollered. "Get in here!"

"Oh my God!" Shock overcame her. In a panic, she turned and took off running down the hallway.

"Aspen!"

7

Declan took a long sip of his chilled beer, trying to watch the baseball game that was on the television. It was in the tenth inning, looking like it was going into the eleventh. He should have been more enthused about the game, but he just couldn't get in to it.

Aspen.

She was on his mind, and he didn't know why he was still contemplating doing a background search on her. He'd done it to everyone who lived in his building and any female he'd fooled around with in the past. Hell, between him and Mac, they'd probably checked out half the city between the two of them.

Being cops made it hard to trust anyone. His experience as a SEAL left him only trusting his men, those he knew had his back. The world was cruel, and he knew it from firsthand experiences.

But with Aspen, there was something deep in her eyes that just didn't sit well with him.

As if she were haunted by something.

He pushed off the couch and stalked into his home office. He sat at his desk and moved the mouse to awaken his sleeping computer.

He'd run the check.

Then he'd feel better.

It would settle all doubts about her.

Placing his beer on the desk, he logged in to the secure website and paused. The cursor blinked steadily in the blank spot for 'name'. He blew out a deep breath and typed in hers.

Aspen Hale.

The cursor moved to the slot for 'address', and he filled in what he knew. He knew her age but was unaware of her birthdate. He filled in as much of the form as he could with the information he knew about her.

Memories of their date came to mind, and he thought of their conversations. She had been vague on her answers about where she'd grown up and her life. Her answers were almost as if they were scripted.

He held the mouse over the 'submit' button and froze. He was unsure why he had a sinking feeling about doing this background on her.

A growl escaped him as he clicked the mouse. He leaned back in his chair, running his hand along his face.

It was a simple background check.

Usually the system took a few minutes to search and compile the data on the target. Tonight, it dinged right away.

"That's strange," he murmured, sitting back up and taking in the information on the screen. It confirmed the basic information he had entered.

Aspen Hale, 29 years old

African-American female

Parents: deceased. MVA accident

No siblings

No family

No college

Grew up in Arizona

Odd jobs through the years

He read the rest of the report. She'd moved around after her parents had died when she'd been nineteen. Since their deaths, the report stated she'd lived in a few states and changed location every year or two with the most recent being South Carolina.

Alarms were still blaring in the back of his mind. This information was too cut and dried. He glanced at his phone, wanting to speak to her. He knew it was late but he just wanted to hear the sound of her voice. If he could get her to open up about herself, then maybe he could let this uneasy feeling he had go.

He grabbed his phone and swiped the glass screen.

He searched through his contacts, passing numbers of countless women he knew he could call on and they'd be at his apartment within the hour.

But none of them appealed to him.

He wanted Aspen.

He hit her number and put the phone to his ear. The sound of ringing greeted him as he stood from his desk and made his way back to the living room.

"Hello?" her soft voice greeted him.

A small smile graced his lips, and he imagined her lying in her bed.

"Hey," he murmured, taking a seat on the couch. He stretched out, ignoring the game still playing on the television.

"Declan," she breathed.

His eyes closed briefly, him loving the sound of his name on her lips. During their night together, she had screamed it quite a few times. He had the sudden urge to want to make her scream it again.

"I hope I'm not waking you."

"No, you're not. It's a little late. You know what they call these type of phone calls?" She chuckled.

His cock stiffened at the husky sound of her laugh.

He grinned, thinking she was right. It was after eleven at night. He wasn't sure if it was that type of call, but he wouldn't be opposed to making it one.

Just hearing her voice had the doubts in the back of mind disappearing. He was going crazy.

He could admit it.

He'd never pondered over a woman before.

Usually, the women he messed with knew up front that he wasn't the committing type. He just wanted a little harmless fun between the sheets.

The vision of Aspen's face as she climaxed had him wanting more.

He craved her.

"If you want it to be, it can be."

His heart skipped a beat at her quick intake of breath. Was she thinking about him as he'd been obsessing over her?

"And if I were to say I wanted it to be," she said, "then what?"

He paused, running a hand across his chest, thinking of an answer. He was sliding down a slope into unknown territory. He had said no strings, and she had agreed.

But the passion between them was too hot to let it fizzle out.

Mac had found the woman for him, maybe this was Declan's chance to find his. Sarena was good for Mac. Declan had instantly seen the change in his friend. The night she'd disappeared, Mac had just about gone nuts.

Aspen may have agreed to a one-night stand, but deep down he knew that wasn't the real Aspen.

"Then I would say I know a great all-night diner that has some good food," he responded, putting his offer on the table. He didn't have to go in to work tomorrow. He was only on call for any situations that would require SWAT.

He reached down and had to adjust himself. His cock, having a mind of its own, was stiff and straining at his sweatpants. He bit back a groan, knowing it was demanding relief.

"Well then, Sergeant Owen, I would ask how soon until you could get here?"

Nervousness filled Aspen as she waited for Declan to arrive. This was all new territory for her. She'd had relationships in the past, but never just sex.

Never a one-night stand.

She was just going to have to get used to her new life.

Get used to meaningless sex.

But the night with Declan hadn't been meaningless.

It had meant something to her. She'd keep those feelings close to her. She didn't know what the future may hold, and if this was all she could have, then she'd grab on to it and never let go of the memories he was giving her.

She laughed at the brazen way she had acted on the phone when he'd called.

"Hussy," she murmured, running her hand over her hair for the thousandth time. She had chosen a cute skirt and low-cut top for their late date. She picked off a few invisible bits of lint from her skirt.

She knew he had called it a date and going out to eat, but she also knew what would be on the table.

Sex.

Hot, sweaty, life-altering sex.

The kind of sex that left you sore the next day.

She wanted it again, and again and again.

Her nipples pushed painfully at her bra with the memories of the last time she had been with Declan. Her core clenched with just the thought of that man's tongue on her neck, her nipples, and buried in her pussy.

"Goodness." She gasped, waving a hand in front of her face. *Calm down.* She couldn't answer the door totally aroused so willed herself to regain some control, thinking of anything but Declan, but that was almost impossible since he was currently on his way. "Think of something else, Aspen."

She reached for the remote and turned the television on to try to distract herself.

It didn't work.

The beams from headlamps flashed across her front window, highlighting the room.

He was here.

She bit her lip and tried to will her heart to stop racing. She stood from the couch and smoothed down her skirt, hoping she wasn't too overdressed—there were only so many times she could wear heels. Working in a library sure wasn't one of them. Restocking returned books and processing new ones that arrived called for comfortable clothes and footwear.

A knock sounded at the side door. She made her way over and brushed the curtain to the side.

Declan.

A smile graced her lips as she opened the door.

"Hey." She leaned against the jamb, taking him all in. His size would be intimidating, but for her it was a major turn on. Her fingers had discovered every inch of his body, and not an ounce of fat could be found.

"Hey, yourself." His deep voice sent shivers down her spine.

"Please, come in. I just need to grab my keys and purse." She waved him inside, shutting the door behind him. She brushed around him and scurried toward the living room. She gasped as his hand clamped down on her wrist.

He forced her body toward his, and she widened her eyes.

He crushed his lips to hers. She groaned, opening her mouth to him, his tongue thrusting forward. His hand gripped her face, anchoring her to him while he thoroughly kissed her.

It was hard and wet.

The evidence of his arousal pressed on her belly. She leaned into him, and his free hand slid along the curve of her back to settle on the swell of her ass.

He reached down and picked her up. Her legs automatically wrapped themselves around his waist, and he carried her toward the living room.

His mouth had yet to leave hers. He maneuvered his way into the dark room, only lit by the light from the television.

She tore her mouth from his and opened her eyes, finding his locked on her. Her breaths were coming fast, making it hard for her to form a single word.

He lowered her to the floor without saying a thing. She stood in front of him, still pressed up against him. The feel of his hard body flush to her soft one left her wanting to feel him on her naked. She didn't want anything to separate the feel of their bodies close to each other.

Her troubles and worries forgotten, she became lost in Declan's eyes. The feral look in them was proof that they wouldn't be leaving the house.

At least not for a while.

She couldn't break the heated stare if someone paid her. His hands slid down and disappeared beneath her skirt. The callouses on his palms gliding along the soft skin of her thighs and hips had her body trembling.

"Declan," she breathed.

He slid her panties from her body.

Without a word, he slowly disrobed her. Moisture seeped from between her folds as he took his time in taking off her clothes, leaving her to stand in front of him in nothing but her heels.

"Beautiful," he murmured, taking in her full form.

Her nipples stood at attention, begging for the feel of his mouth and tongue. He leaned forward, putting his face into the crook of her neck. His tongued bathed her skin, burning a trail along her neck toward shoulders. She gripped his shirt, trying to keep her knees from going out.

He took his time in tasting her, kneeling before her to allow his tongue to make its way to her breasts. She threaded her fingers into his hair as he sucked her breast into his hot mouth. She cried out, wanting to beg him to put her out of her misery.

She needed him deep within her.

Fast and hard.

But by the way he was taking his time, licking and nipping her body, he was about to torture her.

8

The moment Aspen had opened the door, all plans of going out to the diner had gone out the window. An animalistic urge filled him.

He had to have her.

He pushed her down onto the couch, needing to taste all of her. Aspen's soft breasts were a favorite of his. Hell, everything about her was his favorite.

Her smile, her breasts, her pussy, and her ass.

Her skin was soft and sweet, but he wanted her true essence on his tongue. He stood and kicked his shoes off. He removed his clothes in record speed before kneeling on the floor in front of her.

"I thought we were going to go out to get something to eat." She gasped as he brought her to the edge of the couch and spread her legs wide for him.

In the low light, he could see her slickness coating her labia.

She was ready for him.

A growl escaped his chest, and he ran a finger along her slit. He pulled back his finger glistening with her arousal. Her eyes were locked on him while he slowly licked his fingers clean.

Her taste exploded on his tongue.

"I have my snack right here," he murmured, covering her pussy with his mouth.

She cried out, arching her back off the couch.

He plundered her soaked core then dove his tongue between her folds, tasting her sweetness. Her taste was addicting. He wanted it all. He ran his tongue along the full length of her pussy, ending with her clitoris. He suckled her little bundle of nerves into his mouth. Her nails dug into his shoulders as he feasted on her.

He took his time, drawing her close to orgasm, teasing her, swirling his tongue around her nub before dipping into her core. Her juices coated his face, and he continued his torturing of her.

"Declan!"

He introduced a single finger into her channel. His free hand chose to explore, sliding up along her soft belly and landed on her plump breast that filled his large hand to capacity.

He was good at multitasking, and right now, he wanted to ensure that both hands were occupied.

Hers gripped his hair tight to the point where a

slight stinging sensation prickled on his scalp. He smiled and latched on to her clit, introducing a second finger inside her, stretching her. He pinched her taut nipple with his other hand.

"Good God," she cried out.

He increased the pace of his fingers. She thrust her pelvis forward as he teased her. Her muscles tightened around him, and she let loose a scream. Her pussy walls tightened on his fingers, but he refused to pause, wanting to wring this orgasm out of her. Her legs clamped down on his head, and she rode the waves of her release. "Declan!"

She chanted his name, her legs finally releasing his head. He chuckled, her body relaxing back on the couch. He took his time lapping up her release. He pulled his soaked fingers from her and licked them clean.

"Come here," he growled.

There was no way this was ending now. She didn't resist when he pulled her to him, turning her away from him. She knelt on the floor with her stomach braced on the couch. He reached for his jeans and withdrew the foil packet and quickly sheathed his throbbing member.

He lined up the blunt tip of his cock with her soaked entranced and thrust forward hard, eliciting a shout from both of them.

He gripped her hips tight and paused, trying to catch his breath.

"Aspen," he ground out, pulling back and thrusting hard again.

She cried out as he repeated the motion. He couldn't help himself.

This time would be hard and fast.

They had all night for slow and passionate.

"Yes."

The sounds of her cries of pleasure fueled him, and he continued to pummel her slick opening with his hard length. He shot his hand out and entwined his fingers in her hair, anchoring her to him, his hips increasing their pace.

Faster.

He couldn't get enough of her. He needed to be deeper. Her tight channel gripped him as he pushed forward. The sounds of his balls slapping against the meat of her ass filled the air. He tightened his grip on her hair, and then came the familiar tingling sensation seated deep in his balls.

The air grew heavy with the aroma of sex, and it was the best damn scent Declan had ever smelled.

"Aspen, play with your clit," he demanded, needing her to release again. He wanted her to come on his cock this time. He dug his fingers into her skin, losing control. His hips were on autopilot. His gaze locked on the sight of his cock disappearing into her. Her ass shook with each of his hard thrusts, and he grunted his satisfaction.

She did as he commanded. The feeling of her fingers working her clit had him groaning. She buried her face into the couch and cried out. Her muscles clamped down on him, and he roared, his release shooting out of him.

Her muffled cries of passion echoed through the air. His breaths were coming hard and fast as he slammed into her.

He blinked a few times, unable to believe how quick they had gone from zero to one hundred the minute he'd stepped foot in her house.

His semi-soft cock was still buried deep inside her, and he took her all in. It had to be one of the most beautiful sights he'd ever seen.

He willed his heart to slow down and ran a hand along her back, still needing to touch her.

"I didn't hurt you, did I?" he asked, afraid he had been too rough in his taking of her.

"Hmmm?" Her face was still buried in the couch cushion. Her head popped up from the pillows, her dark hair falling around her shoulders.

He regretted having to withdraw his length from her warm cocoon.

She turned her toward him. He leaned back to give

her room to twist around. A crooked smile graced her lips, and she shook her head.

"I asked if I hurt you?" He leaned in to place a small kiss on her lips.

A genuine smile spread across her face. "No."

"Good." He stood and grabbed her. He tossed her over his shoulder and carried her off to the bedroom.

"I promised you a meal and I always come through on my promises," Declan announced, holding open the door to the diner.

"Well, I'm famished," she giggled, walking through. "Somebody caused me to work up quite an appetite."

He growled and pulled her under his arm. They waited for the hostess to come greet them. This was the most relaxed she had felt in a long time. Even with only short spurts of sleep, she felt refreshed, almost like a new woman.

"Just two this morning?" A young teenage girl came over to greet them.

"Yes, ma'am." Declan nodded, not letting Aspen go.

She was comforted by the feel of him by her side. In the back of her mind, she knew this would be temporary, but she blocked that thought. She would bask in the feeling of a semi-normal...whatever this was between her and Declan.

"Follow me." They trailed behind the young woman over to a booth. "Is this okay?"

"It's fine. Thank you." Declan bobbed his head at her as Aspen slid into the booth.

She gasped when he slid in next to her.

"What are you doing?" She chuckled.

The hostess handed them the menu with the promise of their waitress coming soon. She quickly took their drink orders and disappeared.

"I want you within reach of me." He stretched his arm out along the back of the booth. They had been given a back booth where they were in the corner and could look out into the entire restaurant.

Her stomach clenched at his words. She leaned into the crook of his arm and reached for his face. She guided his lips down to meet hers in the softest of kisses.

She opened her eyes and met his green ones.

"I thought you were going to say something cheesy about not wanting your back to the restaurant."

He laughed, placing his arm around her.

"You know that's what they always say in the movies," she said.

"Well, there is that, too." He grinned.

She was enamored by his relaxed features. Her

pulse sped up at his smile, and her heart longed to be able to just spill the beans about herself. Throughout the night when they weren't wrapped up in each other, they'd talked. She'd learned much about him and had to hold back and recite what she was taught about her new self. She ached to tell him about her real life, her real past, and what she had come to be.

But she couldn't.

She knew he was a good cop, a former Navy SEAL. If she couldn't trust someone like him, who would she be able to trust?

She already knew what US Marshal Ball would say.

No one.

"So what's good here?" She pulled back away from him to grab her menu. They hadn't left the cocoon of her home and bed to just to go make out in a public restaurant. She had offered to cook breakfast for them, but Declan insisted on keeping his promise.

They pored over the menu together, with him pointing out what he normally ordered. She widened her eyes at the amount of food it included and shook her head.

"I get it every time. It's good food for your soul." He sat with his arm along the back of the booth.

Her eyes were drawn to his hand patting his rock-hard abdomen.

"Yeah, but it would be food going directly to my ass." She rolled her eyes and finally decided on something to eat.

"All the more you should order what I get," he growled low.

She whipped her head to him and met his laughing eyes.

"Hell, no. It's big enough as it is," she muttered, trying to act offended, but she knew he had an infatuation with her plump ass. She had a bite mark on her right cheek to prove it.

"I'm just saying—"

"Dec?" a male voice called out, grabbing both of their attention.

Aspen watched as a tall, muscular man who had to be ex-military came forward with a short, brown-skinned female attached to his arm.

"Mac." Declan stood and greeted the newcomer in a manly hug. He almost seemed nervous around the couple.

Interesting.

"Who's your friend?" Mac's eyes didn't miss a beat as they turned to her.

She swallowed hard and scooted from the table.

"Mac, this is Aspen. Aspen, this is my best friend, Mac and his fiancée, Sarena." Declan made short introductions.

"Nice to meet you." Aspen gave a small smile and held out her hand.

Mac's eyes were curious and guarded, while Sarena had a shit-eating grin on her face while taking Aspen's hand.

"Why don't you guys join us. We haven't ordered yet," Aspen said.

"I'm sure they will want to eat alone—"

"We'd love to join you," Sarena replied, scooting into the booth.

Aspen didn't miss the tense look between Mac and Declan when they took their seats. She didn't understand: if they were best friends, why the tension?

Her smile faded as different scenarios came to mind.

She knew they hadn't promised each other anything, but then she began to wonder if maybe Declan had someone else.

Their first dinner had been set up.

They'd had sex at her place.

When he'd left, he hadn't asked for her number until they'd run into each other again.

They'd had sex again...at her place.

That would only make sense. He must have another woman.

The waitress decided to show up at that time to grab their orders before she disappeared again.

"So, how long have you two been dating?" Mac asked, settling back against the booth.

"We're not," both said in unison.

She darted her eyes to Declan, but he was in the middle of a staring standoff with his friend. She turned to Sarena who just shrugged.

"There's no need to grill them, Marcas," Sarena said, patting her man on the leg, clearly trying to break the tension. "It's none of our business."

"I just asked a question," Mac said, breaking the stare-off to look at Sarena before turning his attention back to Declan. "Imagine my surprise at stepping into the diner and finding my best friend getting cozy with a woman he's never mentioned to me before."

Aspen's muscles stiffened, her theory growing stronger in her mind by Mac's reaction to her. She didn't know which way this conversation was going to go and didn't want to be the subject of an argument between friends.

She wasn't worth it, and knowing the US Marshalls, they would probably be moving her soon.

No use in two friends arguing. She would just go. She grabbed her purse and blew out a deep breath. "Look, I'll just take my food to go—"

"No."

9

Declan narrowed his eyes on his longtime friend. He was truly at a loss for words for how Mac was acting toward Aspen. It shouldn't matter that he'd never mentioned her; it was blatantly disrespectful the way Mac was behaving.

Aspen had finally relaxed around him. The guarded look in her eyes had disappeared, and now, two minutes in Mac's presence and her walls were back up.

"If you must know, I hadn't mentioned Aspen because this is only the second time we've been out together," he said through clenched teeth. His protective nature was rising, wanting to shield Aspen from his friend.

"But you both just said you weren't dating." Mac's eyebrow lifted.

"We have to eat."

He could feel Aspen's tension brimming from her,

but he refused to let her run off. His gut feeling told him that if she walked out of the diner now, he'd never see her again.

And that wasn't going to happen.

Mac nodded, but Declan could see the questions in his friend's eyes. They would have a different conversation soon, not in front of the women. He didn't want to announce to the entire restaurant that they'd slept together twice and this was only their second date.

No, what happened between him and Aspen was their business.

Their food arrived, breaking some of the tenseness in the air. He moved his eyes to Aspen. She had withdrawn; her eyes were lowered and focused on her food.

He bit back a curse.

"So what do you?" Sarena asked Aspen.

"I work at the County Library. I'm a library assistant," Aspen responded.

The girls began to make idle conversation, but Declan didn't hear any of it. His attention was focused on Mac.

"We have drills starting tomorrow. Are you ready?" Mac asked.

"Always," he replied. Their drill training was to ensure that the team remained the best. It was a few days of training practice where they trained in full gear. Their drills included practicing building entry, takedowns, and search-and-rescue. These training days were to make sure they remained sharp when out on calls.

"So where are you from?" Sarena asked.

"Arizona."

"I've never been there before. I would love to go there sometime." Sarena glanced at him and arched her eyebrow before setting down her fork. "Okay. I have to ask, because I know Marcas is not going to rest until he knows. How did you two meet?"

Declan turned to find Aspen with a small smile on her lips. Their eyes connected, and he could feel the effect of her smile on him. A giggle escaped her, and before he knew it, she fell into a full fit of hilarity. His lips curved up in a smile as he watched her sit back laughing.

"What did I say?" Sarena laughed some more, her eyes switching between Aspen and Declan.

"Well, if you must know..." Aspen paused, trying to gain control of herself. She pushed her hair behind her ear and finally held back her giggles. "A blind date."

"What?" Sarena and Mac echoed, shock registering in both their voices.

Declan could feel his friend's gaze on him and knew Mac would bust his balls about this. He turned and found even Mac holding back a chuckle.

"Okay, let me explain." Declan coughed, trying to

get a handle of the situation. He pushed his empty plate away from him and quickly wiped his mouth with his napkin. He didn't want Mac or Sarena to think he had to be fixed up with blind date to find a woman.

He didn't want to lose his man card.

"Yes, I'd like to hear an explanation on this one," Mac drawled, settling back against the booth and draping an arm around Sarena's shoulders.

"Evie had been after me for a few weeks to meet her friend. She said her friend just moved to town and she trusted me to take her friend out on a date," he began.

"She had been hounding me, too. You'd have to know Evie. She can be quite persuasive," Aspen cut in, glancing at him. "She actually had me feeling sorry for Declan before we even met. I just figured if Evie had to fix her neighbor up—"

"Hey." He tugged on her hair.

Declan Owen never needed to be fixed up.

"I was thinking the same thing," he admitted with a laugh. "When she said that her friend worked at the library with her, I imagined some mousy little nerd—"

"Hey!" Aspen swatted him with her arm and laughed.

"You two are cute together." Sarena sighed, leaning into Mac. "Aren't they, Marcas?"

Declan took a sip of his drink, and his eyes met Mac's. He knew they would be having a different conversation soon.

The waitress stopped by the table, interrupting them, and dropped off the checks. Declan reached for them, but Mac snatched them up.

"My treat," Mac announced, glancing down at the slips.

"No—"

"I said I got it," Mac cut him off, holding his hand up as he reached for his wallet.

"Hey, I'm going to run to the restroom," Aspen murmured.

"I'll go with you," Sarena chimed in.

Both Declan and Mac stood to allow them to scoot out of the booth. They watched the women walk away, before turning to each other.

"Look, Mac," he began, running hand through his hair as they took their seats again.

"I find it funny that you busted my balls when I first started my relationship with Sarena. Imagine my surprise that I find you here on a breakfast date with a woman you've never even mentioned to me."

"Listen, Mac. It just happened, but there is nothing to our relationship."

"Nothing?" Mac cocked an eyebrow.

"We came to agreement. Neither of us is expecting

anything. We are just having a little fun. She knows what this is. I think that is the only reason she's with me right now."

"Really?"

"And why do you have to be an ass to her? I've never treated Sarena with anything but respect," he lowered his voice, noticing a few looks thrown their way from other patrons in the diner.

The first time he'd met Sarena had been in the Emergency Room of the local hospital. He'd been in pain and was pissed at getting shot. She'd stormed in the room and set him in his place. Since that moment, he'd had nothing but respect for her. She was good for Mac.

"I wasn't an ass to her," Mac denied with a shake of his head. "I would never be disrespectful to a woman. Especially someone in a relationship with my best friend."

"I'm not even sure we're going to classify this," Declan murmured.

"Well, anyway. Have you checked into her? Something is off about her. Her eyes are haunted, as if she's carrying secrets."

Declan's eyes flew to Mac's, and he wasn't surprised that Mac had picked up on it, too. He'd tried to ignore the warnings in the back of his mind, and had put them away as him being paranoid. But if Mac had sensed something was off, then Declan knew he wasn't crazy.

"Yeah. It came back clean."

"There is something—"

"Don't worry about it. No need to try to decipher her. She's who she says she is." He held up a hand to cut off his friend. Maybe the long life in the Navy and law enforcement was making them both paranoid.

Aspen was a beautiful woman who made him smile. He glanced up, and his eyes met hers as she and Sarena made their way back to the table. His cock stiffened. Somehow he'd have to get this woman out of his system.

She could be dangerous.

"So, how's the wedding planning coming?" he asked, changing the subject.

"Speaking of wedding planning," Sarena said, arriving back at the table, turning to him. "I have a few things I need the best man to do."

Aspen sighed and wrapped herself in her plush robe. It was late at night, and she didn't even feel sleepy. She was still quite wired from her day. After breakfast with Declan and his friends, he had taken her back home, and somehow they had ended up back in bed again.

Her core clenched as memories of him braced over her came to mind.

She had to get him out of her head.

They couldn't have a future.

She walked out of her bathroom and went into her bedroom. Being hidden in South Carolina was driving her crazy. She wanted to go back to her life. It had been a good one. She missed her parents and her friends. She needed to know how her family was doing.

It just wasn't fair how the US Marshals had burst in her house and taken her away.

"They didn't say I couldn't be on the internet." She grabbed her laptop off her bed. She walked into the living room and flopped down on the couch. It was explained to her when she was put in witness protection that she could no longer have any contact with family members.

Nothing.

But they didn't say she couldn't stalk them from afar on the internet. They did allow her to have a computer, but it was forbidden for her to be on any form of social media.

She tucked her feet beneath her and reached for the remote to the television. Needing some background noise, she flicked the television on. She flipped open the laptop and waited for the computer to boot up. Her heart raced with just thinking of what she'd find on the internet.

"Here's goes nothing..."

The internet opened. She typed in Ray's name, and countless stories returned. A gasp escaped her, and she read the first story.

Ray Acosta, former CFO of Irwin Enterprises, was indicted on charges of murder, embezzlement of two hundred million dollars, conspiracy, money laundering ...

Her gaze flew along the words as she continued reading. She clicked to another news outlet and gasped again.

Ray Acosta, former CFO of Irwin Enterprises, indicted on multiple charges. He is facing a life sentence along with one hundred and fifty years in prison...

She closed her eyes briefly, still unable to believe that the person who was close to her family would do something like this.

She moved the cursor to the search bar and hesitated. Since she'd been in witness protection, she hadn't searched herself. She had been warned against it, but at the moment her emotions were flying high and she needed to know what had been told to her parents. She knew they had faked her death, but it wouldn't prepare her for what she found.

Tears filled her eyes from the multiple articles covering her death.

Irwin Enterprises founder and CEO Mason Irwin's only daughter, Aspen Irwin, was killed in a horrific car crash, while driving late at night...

She brushed back the tears. The story went on to say an eighteen-wheeler had crashed into her car, killing her immediately.

She clicked on another of the local news channels in her old city. The waterworks burst forth—images of her parents at the funeral. Her father held her mother to his chest as she cried.

Her fingers had a mind of their own and clicked on a video link. She blinked through the tears, the video showing her parents leaving the gravesite and walking toward a waiting black limousine.

"A sad day today for business tycoon, Mason Irwin, as he buried his only child today. Such a sad turn events from having his best friend and longtime business partner, Ray Acosta, indicted on charges from stealing from his empire to now having to bury his child..." a news anchor's voice droned on.

Aspen closed her eyes and let the tears flow. She cried for the pain that was etched on her parents' faces. Growing up, she'd never seen her father cry. He was always a strong man who had been firm raising her, but had a heart of gold. She knew as a child that she was a daddy's girl and he was wrapped around her little finger. She'd never taken advantage of it either. She'd always wanted to prove to him that she was just as strong as he was and yearned to make him proud of her.

But to see her father hold her mother with tears streaming down his face broke her.

Everything had been taken from her.

Her body was racked with sobs, and she just sat on her couch and cried.

Her father had always instilled in her that life would never be fair, but this was just going too far.

She wished there was a way she could reach out to them. Angrily, she wiped the tears from her face and vowed that she'd do what she could to stay safe so she could testify against the man who had stolen her life.

Ray Acosta would pay for what he had done to her, her family, and the countless victims who were affected by his embezzling from the corporation.

Her fingers flew across her keyboard as she pulled up another website. There were just a few other things that she had to check on.

10

It was a scorching hot day to be running drills, but it was necessary. Declan was dressed in the normal tactical gear that he wore when they went out on real calls. They practiced as if they were really going out for live calls.

His body was weighed down by his ballistics vest, weapons, and tools. On his head was his protective helmet, and the only thing he chose to do different today was his face mask. No need to wear the mask for drills.

He leaned on the fence in front of him and watched Brodie, the team's entry man, run through his target shooting drill. His body stiffened—a presence came to stand beside him.

"Her record is too clean," Mac announced, resting his arms on the fence.

"I told you I had already run a check on her,"

Declan growled, turning to Mac. "I told you I had already looked into her. She's fine."

"Declan—"

"I don't need you snooping on me and the woman I'm involved with," he snapped, glaring at his longtime friend.

Mac was a hound when it came to something he set his sights on.

"Look, I'm just trying to watch out for you," Mac growled, pushing off the fence.

Declan could feel eyes on them as they stood facing each other. "Don't worry about me. I can take care of myself," he snarled.

Off in the distance, his name was called, interrupting the tense moment between him and Mac. Without a word, he brushed past Mac and stalked away toward the entrance to the obstacle course.

"Hello, Sergeant Owen. You know the drill," the obstacle course coordinator said upon approach.

"Thanks, Bill."

Bill handed him the weapon Declan was to use. He gripped the MP5, feeling somewhat comforted by it. He did a quick check of the weapon to ensure it was ready for use. It was one of his favorites because of the ease of use and extremely reliable when they had to go in hot.

"Are you satisfied with the weapon?" Bill asked, standing by him as he inspected it.

"Sure am," he grunted, reloading the magazine. He reached for his sunglasses from the pocket of his cargo pants and put them on. "I'm ready."

Shooting things when he was upset always helped lighten his mood.

Bill called out that Declan was ready and to ensure all coordinators were off the course.

"Sergeant Owen, you may begin," Bill announced.

Declan gripped the weapon in his hands and brought it up close to him. He steadily aimed it and entered into the course. He narrowed his eyes, on high alert for the targets to jump out at him. He walked down the main path of the fake town and instantly went into his hunter mode.

Time spent in the Navy had prepared him for any situation such as the ones that SWAT was called out to handle.

He tapped into his anger when the targets began to show. With his precision, he hit the targets while running through the course. He didn't miss a bull's-eye. His bullets hit directly in the middle of the target.

His feet moved on their own accord as he confidently made his way through the entire course. Bad guys appeared from behind closed doors, parked cars, and on the roofs of the fake buildings. He didn't hesitate in unloading his bullets into them.

His anger grew with the thought that Mac couldn't accept what he had told him about Aspen and their relationship. He released a growl and shot the last target, again hitting the bull's-eye in the center. He had moved through the course too fast and wanted to continue. His anger was still boiling in his chest.

Maybe he'd go to the shooting range later.

Cheers and shouts echoed through the air, and he walked back through the course. His breaths were coming fast. He made his way back to the entrance.

"Shit, Declan. You got a perfect!" Iker slapped him on the back as he arrived. His team mates surrounded him, and he handed the weapon back to Bill.

"Remind me not to get on your bad side." Zain chuckled.

"Well, men..." Declan began, taking his glasses off. He ignored Mac. At the moment, he was afraid if he said anything else, he'd say something he'd regret. Instead, he turned to his team and focused on them. "One day, you, too, could be as good as Declan Owen," he finished.

They all scoffed and snickered at him. He tried to act as if he wasn't bothered by Mac's words as the guys joked. Ashton's name was called for him to go next.

"Not sure how I'm going to follow Declan." Ashton shook his head, moving over to the entrance.

Declan smirked and leaned against the fence, but he didn't see the course at all.

Aspen's smooth brown skin came to mind. Thoughts of the last time he was with her gripped him. After the breakfast disaster, they had gone back to her house and they'd spent a few hours in bed. He stiffened and knew he had to redirect his thoughts.

He glanced over and found Mac's gaze on him. Declan nodded to him, knowing that deep inside, this was Mac's way of protecting him. They had been through Hell and back when they'd been in the Navy. He knew Mac would take a bullet for him if need be.

Declan had killed for Mac so that he could have a life with the woman he loved.

He blew out a deep breath as the realization came to him. It was if someone had slammed a bat into his solar plexus.

He wanted what Mac had with Sarena.

Sarena had been able to accept Mac with his dangerous job of a police officer and SWAT officer.

Declan had never thought he'd see the day that he would want to settle down. Maybe it was because he was getting older. He blew out a deep breath, thinking it would be nice to have a little Declan or two running around.

He ran a shaky hand along his face, trying to concentrate on Ashton starting the course, but couldn't. He couldn't believe he was standing here contemplating having a future with just one woman.

His gut was telling him that his future was Aspen.

His gut was never wrong and had saved him multiple times when he'd been in the Navy and on a SWAT mission.

But could he trust his heart when it came to Aspen?

Aspen returned her vacuum cleaner to the hallway closet. She had the day off from the library and she was trying to take advantage of the free time to clean her house. The Marshalls hadn't given her a large place, and she'd tried her best to make it homely.

But today, her domain would be cleared from top to bottom. There wasn't much for her to do, and Evie was at work, and Declan...

She let loose a sigh as she fluffed the pillows on her couch. She didn't know what to think about him and what was between them. Any other day in the life of the old Aspen, she would have loved to see where this thing between them was going.

But she was the new Aspen.

Aspen Hale.

A single library assistant who moved around every few years.

Secretly she wished that he did want more from her, but pushed that thought down. Even if he did change his mind, she couldn't.

She didn't even know where she'd be at in six months much less a few years.

Loud rap music filled the air outside her home. She rolled her eyes as it grew louder. She despised her current neighborhood.

"Want-to-be thugs," she murmured and moved over to her front window. She flopped down on her couch and peeked out through the curtain and took in the low-income neighborhood they had stuck her in.

The houses on the street were all similar to hers. Small and compact with neat, tidy yards.

It was the complete opposite of the cushiony suburb where she had grown up in California.

A few kids were out in the yard next door. They stood around the car as the music continued blaring from the speakers.

"Of all the areas they could have chosen, why this one?" she murmured. But she already knew the answer.

They wanted her in an inconspicuous neighborhood where not too many people would notice her coming and going.

Tomorrow she had a meeting with the marshals. According to the text she'd gotten from U.S. Marshal Ball, they would be preparing for her testimony. With Ray being indicted officially, the need of her testimony was getting moved up. The grand jury would be convening within a few weeks, and she would be expected to be there.

She pulled back away from the window and looked around her. The small living room practically sparkled. Determination had set in. After her big cry, she vowed that she wouldn't let her current situation get her down.

Once this was over, she didn't foresee herself moving back to California. The southern city of Columbia was growing on her.

She'd find somewhere to start over.

If only her future could include Declan.

Her cell phone ringing broke through her thoughts. She reached over and grabbed it off her coffee table. Declan's name was splashed across the glass screen. She swiped her finger and answered.

"Hello?" she breathed.

"Aspen." His deep baritone voice came through the phone and instantly sent a chill down her spine.

"Hey, you. How was your day?" she asked, trying to make idle conversation.

Come over and fuck me until I can't speak, was what she wanted to say.

But that may not be appropriate. The man was probably on his shift protecting the city. The few times they had been together had left her becoming addicted to him.

"It was okay." He chuckled.

She smiled, loving the sound of his sexy laugh.

"But it could have been better," he added.

"How so?"

"I want to see you."

His admission made her pause. She glanced down at her outfit and cringed. Leggings and a t-shirt were not sexy.

"When?" she asked, knowing she could be ready in twenty minutes.

"Now," he replied.

She turned around and pulled back the curtains, finding a vehicle parked in the driveway.

"I'm not really dressed to go anywhere," she said.

"I'm sure you're beautiful. Come on," he urged.

She bit her lip, unsure what to do. She watched as he stepped out of his car. The kids all turned to him, openly gawking at the white guy by the fancy sports car.

"Okay. I'll be right out." She hung the phone up and slid her feet into her flip-flops and grabbed her purse. She paused by her hallway mirror and realized that she didn't look too bad.

She swiped her keys and walked out the door.

The sounds of the offending music grew louder when she pulled her door shut and locked it.

Her mouth curved up in a smile, and she took him all in. He leaned against the hood of his car. His jeans and t-shirt were molded to him, highlighting his muscular form. Her heart raced with his gaze slowly perusing her body. Her nipples pushed forward under his assessment.

"Hey." She smiled, feeling eyes from the teens in the next driveway. She tore hers away from Declan and met the open stares of the young men standing around the car with the blaring music. "Where's your truck?"

"At home. It's a nice day, and I wanted to take this out one for a spin." He snagged her hand and pulled her to him.

Her breasts crushed onto his chest, and his large hand slid down her back and gently cupped her ass.

She knew what he was doing.

Laying claim to her in front of their observers.

She tilted back her head, her body flush to his. She smiled, and for just a second she imagined she could belong to him. She basked in the feel of her body pressed up against his and his hands on the swell of her ass.

"Really? Where you want to go?"

"Oh, I don't know." He shrugged nonchalantly. "We can just drive around, and I can take you to one of my favorite spots of the city."

"So is this an official date?" she asked quietly. Her breath caught in her chest as she waited for his answer. She could feel the reaction his body was having to her. She shifted and pushed herself into his hard length that was pressed into her stomach. She bit back a moan, trying to keep her mind from diving into the erotic thought of his thick length.

He eyed her for a second before his lips curled up into a lopsided grin.

"Yes, ma'am," he replied with his thick southern drawl. He leaned in and covered her mouth with a quick kiss. "Let's go."

11

"The zoo?" Aspen exclaimed. She turned to Declan and found a wide grin on his face as he parked the car.

"Yes, the zoo. Don't tell me you've never been to the zoo before." He cocked an eyebrow at her.

She turned her head away from him and glanced out her window at the parking lot that faced the zoo's entrance.

"Well, of course I have. It's just been a long time since I've been to one." She turned back to him with a puzzled grin. "Seriously? The zoo is one of your favorites places to go?"

He barked a laugh and exited the car. He walked around to her side knowing that he'd confused the hell out of her. He could feel her gaze on him as he ambled around the hood. This was a first for him. He'd never brought anyone here as a date and thought she would enjoy it.

Now he was self-doubting.

"Yes, it is. Where else can I go and see the king of the jungle?"

Her musical laughter filled the air, and she placed her hand in his. He pulled her from the car and wrapped his arm around her. Shutting the door, he pushed her back against his vehicle.

"I think it's cute. I was expecting something like a shooting range or something." She giggled.

Her small hands slid up his chest and locked together behind his neck. He let loose a growl and swooped in and met her lips in a sweet kiss.

Declan should have known better. The minute his lips pressed up against hers, sweet went out the window. He pushed his tongue past her slightly parted lips and was a lost man. He angled his head to deepen the kiss. Her fingers gripped the hair at the nape of his neck while a moan erupted from her.

He tore his lips from hers, panting. If he didn't be careful, they'd both be arrested for indecent exposure in public.

"Well, I didn't even think of the gun range." He chuckled, brushing one last kiss on her swollen lips.

"Maybe date number two?"

He took in the relaxed look on her face. Her smile was genuine, and she literally seemed happy. It was a start. If this was all it took to please her then he'd start planning a million little dates.

"Consider it done." He smiled, stood back from her, and offered his hand. He had to will his cock down. It was pressing hard against his jeans, and it wouldn't do him any good to walk around with an erection around families and children. "So what is the first animal you want to see?" he asked.

They walked up to the payment booth. He took care of the fee and guided her inside the park. She leaned on his arm, and he basked in the feel of her relaxing into him.

"I've always been partial to elephants." She opened up and spoke of how, as a child, she'd been fascinated with the large, intelligent animals.

He tried to contain his shock at the mention of her childhood. "As the lady wishes," he replied.

Aspen lost track of time as they made their way through the beautiful area. She'd forgotten what it felt like to walk carefree without having to constantly look over her shoulder.

Declan, being a gentleman, made her feel safe and secure. The true southern gentleman in him was showing. His hands were constantly on her. From holding her hands, to placing his hand in the small of her back when walking along with her.

"They are so beautiful," she breathed, staring at the lions lounging around in their exhibit. The male, with its large mane, sat beneath a tree taking advantage of the shade that was offered. The animal glanced around, observing the crowd clamoring to get pictures of it.

"Powerful beast." Declan wrapped his arms around her and pulled her back against his hard body.

Aspen sighed, loving the feeling of him pressed close to her. She relaxed, imagining this could last forever.

"Where do you want to go? I think we've seen about everything!" She turned in his arms and glanced up at him.

"We didn't see the bears," he teased.

"Oh my! How could I forget about them?" she exclaimed, jumping in place.

Declan laughed at her and grabbed her hands. She was taken back to her childhood with this date. It had been perfect. She hadn't been to the zoo since her teenage years and had forgotten how much fun one could have there.

"But before we go there, let's stop and grab a bite to eat. There's a great little restaurant not too far from here that serves surprisingly good food considering it's located in a zoo."

"I'm famished." She hadn't realized she'd worked

up an appetite. Her belly chose that moment to make itself known.

Declan cocked an eyebrow, and a giggle escaped her. He must have heard it.

"Yes, let me feed you." The corner of his lips curved up in his infamous, sexy, crooked grin. He wrapped an arm around her shoulders and guided her away from the lion exhibit. His arm stiffened, and he brought them to a halt.

"What is it?" she asked, confused. She tried to follow his line of sight but couldn't see what he was looking at.

"I first thought it was nothing, but now I'm sure of it." Even behind his sunglasses, his eyes had darkened, focused on whatever had caught his attention.

Naturally, her body swayed toward him as if it knew he'd protect her.

"What are you talking about?" Even with the warm weather and bright sunrays beaming down on them, a chill still slid its way down her spine. Her heart raced with fear creeping into her chest.

Had they found her?

Was her cover blown?

A million thoughts raced through her head. Every situation the marshals had warned her about came to mind. Her fingers itched to grab her cell, but Declan's arm tightened around her briefly before he turned to her with a small smile on his lips.

"He's gone now. Maybe I'm just being paranoid," he said, but the smile didn't reach his eyes.

She didn't want to press it and cause him to become suspicious of her. The way his eyes scanned the area around them reminded her of the animal they had just observed.

He was no different than the lion.

Declan Owen was a predator. His job required someone who was fearless. She imagined he'd faced killers and the most hardened criminals in his line of duty. The look on his face was certainly one that would make a person think twice about crossing him.

"Okay. Food. You were going to take me to get food," she reminded him, jostling him from his thoughts.

He nodded and entwined their fingers, guiding the way. She released the breath she didn't realize she'd been holding. This was one thing she knew she'd have to report to the marshals. She just hoped it wasn't enough to make them decide to move her.

She was just getting used to Columbia and all that the city had to offer, mainly one SWAT Officer named Declan Owen.

Declan was certain they were being followed. He put on a cool and collected front. He didn't want to alarm Aspen. He hadn't meant to frighten her, but when he'd turned and caught sight of the man staring at her, alarms had gone off. He'd had the feeling someone was tailing them, and that had confirmed it.

They'd yet to figure out who had leaked their names to the Demon Lords. Declan was worried that until they caught the person, he would be at risk. It was his bullet that had slammed into the forehead of their leader, Silas Tyree.

"Thank you for bringing me here." Aspen smiled, walking alongside him. She squeezed the teddy bear he'd bought her from the gift shop. Its fat belly was covered with a red t-shirt with the zoo's name splashed across it.

"Any time." He pulled her close, unable to keep his hands off her.

She buried her face into the bear's neck.

"What shall we name him?" She reared back and looked up at him.

Her eyes were mesmerizing, and he could easily get lost in them.

"Name who?" He'd totally missed what she'd said.

"The bear?" She held the toy up in the air. The brown bear had a crooked smile sewn onto his face. He looked pitiful, but Aspen's face had lit up when she had paused in front of it while it sat on the shelf. He'd instantly picked it up and handed it to her, paying for it. He was glad no one he knew had seen him buy a teddy bear for a woman. He might have lost his man card for that. "He can't not have a name."

The hairs on the back of Declan's neck rose. They were almost out of the zoo. He'd left his service weapon locked up in the glove compartment in his car. His fingers itched to feel the cool, hard steel of his Glock. He casually looked around and didn't see anyone.

But they were there.

His gut had never let him down before.

"I don't know...how about Tom, Henry, Mark—"

"What?" Aspen drew back with a look of horror on her face. Her wide eyes stared at him as if he'd grown another head.

"What's wrong with those names?"

She broke out into a fit of giggles and shook her head, holding the bear against her chest.

"How about Preston?"

They exited the zoo and headed toward the parking lot. The sun had shifted, denoting it was later in the day. He couldn't believe they had spent the better part of the day at the zoo. They'd enjoyed themselves.

There was something bothering him about Aspen. Declan did pick up that every time he'd turned the conversation to her, she'd dodged him or given him answers that seemed like they were perfectly rehearsed. It just didn't settle right with him. At times, the haunted look had appeared in her eyes but disappeared just as quick at it had appeared.

"I think Preston is the perfect name." He laid a kiss on her forehead.

The chill that slid down his spine didn't sit well with him. He knew they were being watched. If he'd been by himself, he'd grab his weapon out of his car and go confront whoever it was, but since he had Aspen with him, he'd just leave and ensure she was safe.

He remained alert, guiding Aspen to the car. His gaze swept the parking lot; he didn't see anything, but the alarms were still going off in his mind. Dusk was upon them, which would make it harder to see. The shadows were growing as they were losing sunlight. There weren't many people in the parking lot, which could be a gift or a curse.

They strode along the walkway, heading toward the car in a comfortable silence. It came into sight, and he breathed a sigh of relief. Once in his car, he'd be able to lose whoever was following them.

"I think he looks like a Preston." She nodded, satisfied on her name choice.

Today was the most relaxed he'd seen her, and it

bothered him that he had the feeling she was hiding something. He loved seeing her so carefree and smiling all day long. He wanted to ensure she was able to remain that way.

"Thank you, Declan. This was so sweet of you. I haven't had this much fun in quite some time."

The seriousness of her look took his breath away.

She *was* hiding something.

"The pleasure was all mine," he admitted. The feeling of dread filled his stomach just as they reached the car. He opened the passenger door and paused, taking in the sight of five men coming from behind the trucks near his car.

"Such a pretty little thing you got there." One of the men stepped forward.

Aspen's gasp filled the air. Declan pushed her behind him, ready to defend her. He narrowed his eyes on them, memorizing everything he could about them. He'd be damned if he'd let anything happen to his woman.

12

Aspen peeked from behind Declan's back and took in the thugs. Her heart raced, seeing that they were completely outnumbered and no one was around to help them. She slowly reached into her purse and pulled out her cellphone. She kept her body hidden behind Declan so the men couldn't see her actions.

She'd have to alert the marshals now.

She didn't have a choice.

"I think you all need to move along here," Declan drawled.

His body was coiled tight, and she knew he was preparing to defend her.

"I think we are good where we are," the leader replied.

The men spread out in front of them.

Aspen quickly slid her finger across the screen of her phone and hit the last text she'd received from US Marshall Ball.

Help, she typed out. She sent the text and focused on the men surrounding them.

"Aspen, get in the car," Declan ordered, his voice cold and hard.

"No, Aspen. Don't," the leader sneered.

A chill slid down her spine at the way he'd pronounced her name. She knew without a doubt they were here for her.

Her cover was blown.

She sent up a prayer that the marshals would get her message before it was too late. She wouldn't be able live with herself if something happened to Declan because of her.

"Get in the car, Aspen," Declan repeated, sliding to the right to allow her to slip inside.

She eyed the men and shifted toward the door.

"Get her!" the leader ordered.

Declan pushed her inside the car. "Glovebox!" he shouted.

Without hesitation, she dove for it. She gripped the handle and pulled it open. The driver's-side door opened, and a thug slid in. She cried out from his grip on her arm. Declan quickly reached inside the car, but he was dragged away from her.

"Let me go!" she screamed.

The sounds of a fight ensued outside the vehicle. She grew frantic seeing the men converge on Declan.

He was hanging in there, swinging his fists, but the four of them were proving to be too much for him. The man's grip tightened on her arm, tugging her across the console between the driver and passenger seats, and she lost sight of Declan. Her gaze landed on Declan's gun.

"Come on, bitch!" the man growled.

She stretched herself and brushed the weapon with her fingers while fighting against her attacker. She surged forward and grabbed it. She'd only ever held a gun a couple of times in her life. Her father had wanted her to know how to protect herself when she moved out on her own.

She cried out as she was dragged from the car. She had to protect herself. If they took her, there was no telling what would happen to herself.

Take the safety off.

She remembered that and flipped it. Wrapped both hands firmly around the handle. Her body hit the ground once he'd hauled her completely from the car. She turned and aimed at his chest and pulled the trigger. Her arms jolted from the force of the weapon.

His body jerked, and he took a step back. His eyes were filled with shock. His mouth flopped open a few times before he crumpled to the ground. With the sound of the gunshot and the echo of sirens making their way to them, curses lined the air.

She stood and aimed the weapon at the frozen men who'd attacked Declan, who was out of her sight.

"Get away from him!" she shouted. Her heart raced, and her hands shook. She didn't think she had it in her to shoot someone else and hit them. Her aim was faltering, but the men apparently didn't want to take a chance with her.

"Let's get out of here. Cops are coming!" one of the men snapped.

"Grab Diesel!"

They began to scramble, and she made her way around the car with the gun still aimed at the men. She caught sight of Declan lying on the ground, and her heart seemed to jump into her throat. The sounds of the sirens grew closer.

"Leave him! We have to go!" the leader spat.

"Declan!" she cried out, flying to his side.

He sat up, his eyes wide and frantic. His face was bruised, and blood trickled from a cut on his forehead and the corner of his mouth. He relaxed when his eyes connected with hers.

"Aspen." He grimaced.

She knelt by him, her lip trembling from trying to hold back her tears. She couldn't let loose now.

A mixture of unmarked cars and police blue-and-white cruisers flew up and parked near them, surrounding the area.

"I'm so sorry," she whispered. Her heart pounded away at the sight of his injuries.

Shouting filled the air as law enforcement swarmed the parking lot.

"There's nothing for you to be sorry for." He pushed himself up to a standing position. He swayed on his feet, and she stood to help him. "I'll take that." He reached for his gun.

She gladly handed it over, unable to believe she'd shot someone. Just the thought that she may have taken a life nauseated her. She couldn't bring herself to look to where the man had fallen. Declan wiped the gun with his top then pulled her near him while he reached in his back pocket.

Uniformed officers approached them, guns pointed at them. Aspen gasped, pressing closer to Declan. His grip tightened on her while he held up his badge.

"Sergeant Declan Owen. SWAT," he announced.

Two officers stood near them, lowering their weapons.

Aspen took in the scene surrounding them. Police and investigators converged on the area. It was like a scene from a movie playing out in front of her. A few uniforms were over on the other side of the car where the man she shot lay. They called out for the EMTs to come to them.

"I'm Officer Cruz." He was tall and of muscular

build. His hair was kept clipped short. His eyes moved back and forth between Declan and Aspen.

She noted that he still kept his weapon in his hands but now it was trained on the ground.

"I'm Officer Reeves," the shorter one said. He, too, kept his weapon in his hands.

Aspen, not feeling too keen on them, stayed by Declan's side.

"We received reports of an attack on one white male and one black female here in the parking lot along with gunshots fired."

"That would be correct," Declan snapped. He looked around as if seeing the chaos for the first time. "We're the victims. Now are you going to take our statements or are you going to stand there with your gun in your hands?"

They both jumped at his tone and put away their weapons. Cruz, appearing to be new, struggled to get his notepad and pen out while Reeves shot him an impatient look.

"May we get the female's name, please?" Officer Reeves asked Declan.

"Aspen. Aspen Hale," Aspen replied, clearing her throat. Her hands grew sweaty as her nerves rose.

Where were the US Marshals?

"And may I ask why you were at the zoo?" Cruz asked, scribbling in his notepad.

"Are you fucking kidding me? What the fuck you think we were doing here?" Declan growled.

The two officer's eyes widened at his snarl. Aspen held back a smirk at their reactions.

Well, duh. They were just leaving the zoo. What did he think people did at the zoo?

"Sorry. So were you leaving or coming to the zoo?" Cruz asked.

"Leaving," Declan replied. He was not even trying to hide his irritation.

Aspen began to feel sorry for the young cop with the way Declan was glaring at him.

"Please describe what happened?" Officer Reeves cut in.

Declan blew out a deep breath and began to recount the story of them leaving the zoo. She leaned her head against his arm as he told their story. When it came to the part about shooting the man, Aspen's heart lodged in her throat. Did Declan just say *he* shot him?

"So you shot the man?" Reeves asked, asking for clarification.

"No, you didn't. I did." Aspen shook her head. She didn't want him to get in any trouble for this. If anyone was to pay for shooting the thug, it would be her.

Aspen's gaze landed on the EMTs lifting a stretcher with the body of the man she'd shot. She swallowed hard, tearing her eyes from the sight of them pulling a white sheet over his face. The other thugs were handcuffed and led to a black van.

This madness needed to end soon, but even after she testified against Ray, her life would still not be what it used to be.

She turned back and caught the two officers glancing at her.

Declan gently turned her to him. His eyes searched hers.

"I think you may be having some memory deficit from the attack. I think you hit your head when he dragged you from the car. I shot the man," Declan said slowly.

"We're going to need both of you to come down to the station," Officer Reeves announced.

"Is this really necessary?" Declan said.

"Sergeant, you know the routine. This involved a shooting with an off-duty officer. Both of you will need to come to the precinct for official statements and questioning." Officer Reeves snapped his notebook shut and returned Declan's stare. "And Sergeant, we will need to confiscate your weapon. Standard protocol."

"Fine. But we go together," Declan agreed. He released the clip before handing the weapon to the officer. Declan dropped both into the evidence bag for them to secure it.

Reeves nodded and motioned for them to

accompany them to a squad car. Declan entwined his fingers with hers and walked alongside her. Aspen was relieved that she wasn't going to be put in handcuffs. She glanced over at Declan's face and knew he wouldn't have taken her being put in the restraints well. A little tick in his jaw jumped.

There were so many people in the parking lot. People taking pictures of the scene, people putting number signs down by evidence. Even Declan's car was being processed. A growl vibrated from his chest when he got a look at his car.

"Hold on. Where do you think you're going?" a familiar voice spoke up from behind them.

They paused, turning to look at the newcomer.

The feds had arrived.

"I'm US Marshal Elliot Ball. What in the hell happened here?" Ball barked, flashing his credentials.

A couple of men in suits joined him. Aspen jumped at the tone of his voice but was still relieved he'd got her message. He'd have tracked her via her cell. His gaze landed on Aspen and dropped to her and Declan's entwined hands.

He stopped next to Aspen, his attention focused on Declan. "Who the hell are you?"

"Sergeant Declan Owen. Since when does an assault in the zoo's parking lot require the US

Marshals?" Declan demanded, tightening his grip on her hand.

"Declan, I can explain." Aspen sighed, turning to Declan, trying to push down the bile that was threatening to force its way up.

"You'll do no such thing, Ms. Hale," US Marshal Ball cut her off, motioning for her to come to him.

He glanced down at his watch, and dread filled her. She knew what that meant.

Her time in Columbia was over.

"It's time to go, Ms. Hale." Ball's voice broke through her thoughts.

She glanced back to Declan, who stood with a confused expression on his face. She turned to him, tears blurring her vision. She reached up to grip his face and made him look at her. His eyes softened once they met hers.

"Thank you," she whispered, her heart slowly breaking. She'd known that eventually this day would come. She'd have plenty of memories of him to take with her. Once again, Ray Acosta had taken everything from her, and this time, he was locked away in a jail cell doing it. "For everything. I'll never forget you."

"Forget me? Aspen, what the hell is going on?" His hand gripped her hip, pulling her close. His gaze shot over her shoulder to the US Marshals standing by to take her away.

"We don't have time, Aspen. We need to go now."

"She's not going anywhere except down to the precinct," Officer Reeves announced, apparently having found his balls. "Either she comes willingly or it'll be in handcuffs."

"You wouldn't dare." Declan moved to stand before her.

Cruz took a step back, but Reeves stood firm where he was.

"On what charges?" Ball demanded.

"Well, if you didn't notice, we have a dead man and we have reason to believe it was Ms. Hale who shot him."

13

Declan paced the small room, infuriated. Once they had arrived at the precinct, the feds had taken Aspen away from him. He didn't know what the hell was going on but he was going to get to the bottom of it. The feds had been closed-lipped on everything.

What the hell do the feds have to do with Aspen?

"You're wearing a hole in the floor," Mac's voice broke through his thoughts.

Declan blew out a deep breath. He was feeling trapped in the small interrogation room. The windowless space was a cliché of television drama shows with its bleak decor and mirror on the wall. The minute he'd arrived, he'd placed a call to Mac who'd appeared immediately. Without a doubt, Mac was the one person he'd call with any problems. "I'm sure she's fine—"

"She's not fine. Those men were going to take her. If it was Sarena, what would you do?" Declan asked,

PEYTON BANKS

cutting Mac off. It was a low blow. This situation was a slightly different from when Sarena had been kidnapped by a powerful gangster who would have killed her to extract revenge on Mac. But for Declan, seeing those men try to abduct Aspen put him in the same mindset that Mac had been in. He would have gladly emptied his clip into every single one of those men. Declan didn't know what she was involved in and didn't care. He'd finally realized what the haunted look in her eyes really was.

Fear and loneliness.

He would be there for her. Erase that sadness from her eyes.

During Mac and Sarena's ordeal, Declan and the rest of SWAT had been right by Mac's side doing everything in their power to get her back.

Mac paused, his eyes darkening as he met Declan's gaze. Their intense standoff was interrupted by the door opening. Captain Spook entered the room, his eyes shifting between Declan and Mac, having picked up on the tension in the room.

"Have a seat, Sergeant Owen," the captain ordered. His commanding presence drove Declan to have a seat next to Mac. He flopped down in the chair and glanced at Mac.

"Sorry, man. That was low," Declan muttered, running a hand along his jaw. Mac was as close to him

120

as a brother, and they'd been through tough times. That didn't give him any right to be a dick.

"Don't worry about it." Mac sniffed.

They turned their attention to the captain.

"Now that you ladies are done with whatever the hell I walked in on, we have important matters at hand," Captain Spook snapped, taking a seat across from them.

Declan sat straight in his chair.

"IRB will be here in any moment. Declan, they are going to be up in your ass since this involved an altercation while you were off duty."

Declan nodded, fully aware of the situation that was coming.

"Now I want to hear from you exactly what happened."

Declan blew out a deep breath and retold the story he had already told the uniforms. Mac's hands balled into fists as Declan got to the part where the men had appeared.

"What has she said?" Mac asked.

"Not much. The feds wouldn't let her say anything. She just said she was sorry and she wouldn't forget me. The feds are taking her." Declan leaned his elbows on the table and gripped his hair in his hands. He squeezed his eyes shut, hating the feeling blossoming in his chest.

Fear.

A strong, comforting hand gripped his shoulder.

Mac.

He'd never been one to experience this before. Not when he was deployed, not on any SWAT call, but the sensation was there, weighing him down. Had he not yelled for her to open the glovebox, she wouldn't have grabbed the gun. The guy she shot would have dragged her off, and there was no telling what they would have done with her.

"Do you think it's anything illegal?" Mac questioned the captain.

Declan raised his head to look at the captain.

"From what I was able to gather from Agent Ball, she's in witness protective custody. After the air is cleared about what happened down at the zoo, I imagine they are going to take Ms. Hale and disappear."

"But the matter comes back to her firing my weapon and killing the suspect. Will she be charged with anything?" Declan was reaching for any reason she would have to stay.

"Doubt it. There were enough witnesses leaving the zoo who saw what happened and called the authorities. She should be cleared from that, and knowing the feds, if they need her bad enough, this will be filled away as a righteous kill and swept under the rug."

"Can I speak with her?" Declan asked. He was dying to see Aspen. She had been shaken up after the ordeal. She'd barely let his arm go once the cops had arrived. His heart stuttered thinking that she was alone and afraid with the feds in the other room.

"Let me see what I can do. Stay right here." The captain glared at him.

Declan knew the look, and if he didn't want to be busted down to traffic duty, he'd keep his ass in the seat.

The captain pushed back his chair and stood. "I'm going to see if I can delay IRB so we can work out what the hell is going on."

Declan and Mac remained silent until the door shut again. Mac blew out a deep breath, standing. It was his turn to pace the floor. His movements were that of a predator. Declan recognized it because it was how they were. That's what made them perfect for SWAT.

"What are you thinking?" Declan asked. He knew when Mac was lost in thought and planning.

"Where was this relationship of yours going?" He turned and faced Declan.

He scowled at Mac and flew from the chair, knocking it over.

"Calm down. I'm asking because I need to know how far in we're going to be."

"I'm all in for her." He clenched his fist.

Mac nodded and walked over to the door. He opened it and stood back while Zain, Iker, Ashton, Brodie, and Miles filed into the room. Each man was decked out in the black fatigues as if prepared to go out on a call. Mac shut the door behind them and moved to stand before them.

His team.

Brothers-in-arms.

He met the eyes of each of his teammates and gave them an appreciative nod.

"Aspen is your woman, then she's one of us," Mac announced.

As always, Columbia Police Department protected their own.

Aspen blew out a deep breath and tried to calm her nerves. Ball sat at the table with her while the detectives sat across from her. They eyed her with distrust on their faces. They'd gone over the story of what happened at least four times.

She'd lost track of time since she'd entered the small interrogation room.

"How did you get Sergeant Owen's gun?" Detective Roth asked, cocking an eyebrow.

She'd seen the look in his eyes before. It was the look of a cop who had already deemed her guilty just because of the color of her skin. As if all people of color were guilty of heinous crimes.

"Right before those men attacked us, Declan made me get in the car and told me to open the glovebox. But before I or he could get it, the men jumped him, and the one I shot—" Her voice ended on a catch. She bit her lip to keep it from quivering.

She'd taken a life.

Her vision blurred, making it hard for her to see. She sniffed and ran a hand across her eyes to wipe the tears before they fell. She wasn't a violent person and because of that man's actions she'd had to protect herself.

There was only one man to truly blame for this.

Ray Acosta.

"And your relationship with Sergeant Owen is what?" Detective Shots asked.

She rolled her eyes. This was the second time he'd asked her the question. He'd only formed it a different way this time. She glanced over at Ball who nodded.

"We've been seeing each other," she replied. She looked him straight in the eye, not caring if she appeared agitated. She was tired, hungry, and worried about Declan. Since arriving at the police precinct, she'd yet to see him. They'd kept them separated, and she was worried that he was still trying to claim that he'd shot the dead guy. "It hasn't changed since the last time you asked me."

Roth let out a snort and tapped his fingers on the table. Nothing she could say was going to change this man's prejudice against her. He was probably counting down the seconds until he could handcuff her and throw her in a jail cell.

"I'm just curious on why, if you are a regular woman dating an officer, the feds have to be here in the room—"

"As I told you, you don't have clearance to know why Ms. Hale has to have a federal agent here," Ball cut off Detective Shots' question. His demeaning tone wasn't lost on any of them in the room. Neither of the detectives' pay grade would allow them the privilege to know the details of Aspen's case. "Now as I told you, there will be no charges against Ms. Hale. It was purely self-defense. You have about ten witnesses who reported those men were assaulting your coworker and trying to drag her off to kidnap her."

"Now see here—"

The door opened, and a tall, older man in a uniform with an air of authority entered.

"Good evening," the man said. His gaze landed on Aspen before he offered his hand to her. "Hello, Ms. Hale. My name is Captain Spook."

She murmured a greeting before sitting back and watching him greet Agent Ball.

The detectives stood from the table, offering their seats to the captain. He sat in his chair, his worn face looking as tired as Aspen felt.

"Ms. Hale, I've recently gotten off the phone with the mayor, and it would seem there will be no charges brought up on the death of the man you shot," Captain Spook announced.

"What?" Shots and Roth echoed simultaneously. Their complaints were silenced with one stern glare from the captain.

Aspen held back a smirk, watching the emotions cross Roth's face. He had wanted to find a reason he could arrest her, but it looked like the feds must have spoken with the mayor.

"Ms. Hale, you are to be released into the custody of the US Marshals." Captain Spook nodded to Ball.

"Thank you, Captain." Ball stood and extended his hand to the captain, who took it.

"Before you go, we have someone who wants to speak to Ms. Hale." Captain Spook stood from his chair.

Aspen already knew without question who would be outside the door waiting for her.

"We don't have time—"

"Please," she whispered, turning her eyes to Ball.

His lips pressed in a firm line before he blew out a deep breath.

"Fine. A few minutes, then we must go."

She nodded and stood, watching as the men filed out the room, ignoring Roth's hard glare as he followed his partner out. Her attention was captured by the sight of a bruised Declan standing by the door.

"You don't have long, Declan. The captain patted Declan on the back. "I'll see what I can do."

"Thanks, Captain," Declan breathed before stepping into the small room. He shut the door and leaned back against it.

Their eyes met as they stood staring at each other.

She bit her lip to keep the cry from escaping her lips then rushed to him. He stepped forward and caught her in his embrace. His strong arms folded around her, and she squeezed him as tight as she could. Sobs escaped her.

"I'm so sorry," she hiccupped. Her face was buried against his chest as the sobs continued.

"You don't have to be sorry," he murmured, his chest vibrating with his words.

The strength of him brought her comfort. She sniffed, regaining control of herself. In his arms she no longer felt alone. In his arms was where she wanted to stay for all time, but there was a certain federal agent not too far away who would prevent it from happening.

"Are you all right?"

She pulled back with a nod. Declan reached up and wiped her tears away with his thumbs.

"As good as I can ever be."

"I'm here for you. You don't have to do this alone." His eyes searched hers.

He cupped her cheek, and she leaned into it, knowing she could trust him.

Her heart skipped a beat. She shook her head slowly, unsure of what to say. How much did he know?

"I've been alone for so long—"

Their conversation was interrupted by the door opening. US Marshal Ball stood in the doorway. His mouth was pressed into a thin line, and he glared at them. Aspen leaned into Declan, not wanting to leave.

"I'm not sure who Captain Spook knows, but it would seem he has called in a favor. Sergeant Owen will be coming with us for the night."

14

"This is a safe house. We'll use it for tonight," US Marshal Ball announced, closing the door. He waved Aspen over to the couch while his partner disappeared into the kitchen.

Declan took in the space. The windows were covered with drapes, and a small couch and love seat faced each other. The decor was plain, but it wouldn't be decorated as if a family lived here. He walked around the room intent on ensuring that this was a safe environment for Aspen.

The car ride had been silent and full of tension. He didn't know what the hell was going on, but she had a lot of explaining to do.

Why the hell would those men be after her?

He turned, cataloging every detail of the house that was visible.

"I hope it's to your liking," Ball drawled, leaning against the wall.

"It will do," he replied, his gaze landing on Aspen.

Her eyes were cast down to the floor, and he bit back a snarl. Her hands were collapsed together in her lap. The look on her face was of a person who had lost everything. He let loose a sigh and moved to her.

She needed him.

Even with them in the room, she seemed alone.

"I trust what is shared with you will be upheld with the strictest of confidence. I looked into you, Sergeant Owen, and you're well-respected in the law community."

"You're damn right I am," Declan said, settling on the coffee table in front of Aspen. He reached for her hand and entwined their fingers.

Her eyes flew to him in shock.

He gave her a tight squeeze to let her know that he was there for her. "Now tell me. What is going on?"

"Aspen has been in the witness protection program. She was the witness of a murder. The person charged with the murder is up for a lot of federal charges. She is the one person who can assure the bad guy is put away for a long time."

Declan glanced at the federal agent. The other one, US Marshal Williams, entered the room.

"I'm going to double-check out back to make sure we're good for the night." He left out the front door and shut it behind him.

Declan returned his attention to Aspen who remained quiet on the couch. He was slightly relaxed knowing the feds were making sure Aspen was protected.

"That sounds like a lot. What happened, baby?" he asked.

She blew out a deep breath and kept her eyes lowered. "My name is not Aspen Hale. My real name is Aspen Irwin, and I'm from California."

"Nice to meet you, Aspen Irwin," he murmured, squeezing her hand.

Her lips tilted up in a small smile, and he was slightly relieved she *could* smile. Her eyes softened when she gazed at him.

"I was at work late one evening. I am—or at least I used to be—a forensic accountant, one of the best. My father runs a Fortune 500 company and asked me to look into some dealings and monies that seemed to have disappeared." Her eyes glassed over as she told her story.

He watched her become lost in the tale. He remained quiet while she continued speaking, not wanting to interrupt her.

"I had figured it out. I couldn't believe who was stealing from my father. He'd worked so hard to get his company to where it was supposed to be, and for me to find out it was his best friend, I was just in shock.

"I went to confront him. I had thought of him as an uncle. He and my father had been as close as brothers, but he chose to turn to the life of crime and stabbed my father in the back."

This started sounding familiar to Declan. He swerved his eyes to the federal agent who crossed his arms in front of his chest and leaned against the wall. He'd remember hearing about something in California about a high-profile case of an executive. He turned back to Aspen. His heart raced, seeing the fresh trail of tears burning their way down her cheeks.

"I should have waited and gone to my father first, but I was just so angry and wasn't thinking. I walked up to his office, and as I was about to push the door open, I heard angry voices. It was slightly open, and I watched Ray shoot that man."

Declan knew the case. It was all over the news. He gazed at Aspen with a new understanding of who she was.

Holy shit.

"Ray Acosta?"

Aspen was shocked Declan knew who she was speaking of. But then, the case had been all over the national news. When she'd first been pulled from her home, she hadn't been able to watch television without seeing his face splashed crossed the screens.

"Yes, he's currently sitting in prison awaiting his trial. We have to keep Ms. Hale alive so she may testify against him," Ball stated, breaking the shocked silence.

"Declan, there's so much I want to say, but—"

"You're not leaving." His tone was hard and clipped.

"You don't get to decide that, Sergeant." Ball's eyes narrowed on Declan's back.

"I have to go," she whispered.

Declan's sharp eyes lingered on her. They softened the longer they stared at each other. Even with the shadow of the bruising appearing on his face, she thought he was the most handsome man she'd ever met. She reached out and cupped his jaw. His shadow of a beard prickled against her hand. "If this was any other time—"

"What are you going to do? Keep moving her from city to city, hiding her?" Declan snapped, turning his attention to Ball.

"That's exactly what we are going to do. My job is to make sure that she stays alive and can testify."

"And after she does that, then what?"

Her breath caught in her throat at Declan's question.

She already knew what she would do. She couldn't

live her life forever staying in protective custody. This was no way to live her life. The money they provided her with wasn't enough to live off of. With her bleak work history, the only jobs she would qualify for would offer minimum wage.

No. She couldn't continue her life like that.

She'd been a damn good accountant and always planned for the what-ifs. She'd taken her own money and hid it far away, and no one had a clue. The government never knew that she'd taken enough of her own money that she'd received from her parents when she'd graduated from college and hid it in offshore accounts.

Aspen had always had a plan. Testify, see her family one last time, and disappear. Ray had ties to dangerous men, and once they found out she was alive, they'd go after her. She'd never be safe here in the States.

She'd have to relocate to another country. Anything to ensure she was safe, she'd be willing to do it, and if starting life on a different continent was the only way, she'd do that, too.

"After she testifies, we'll hide her deep. She'll receive a new identity and will live a quiet life."

Declan ran his hands through his hair and closed his eyes. She stared at him, torn. Her heart was breaking watching the frustration appear on his face.

"She doesn't have to leave yet," Declan stated. He

stood and paced the floor, concentrating on something unseen.

"If you have forgotten, she and you were attacked in a public area. Someone knows she's alive. We have to move her. Tonight."

Aspen jumped at the news they were wanting to relocate her tonight. It shouldn't have been a surprise. They usually moved her under the cover of darkness. She should be used to it by now, but this time, she was losing someone she had come to care for.

"I can protect her." Declan stopped and faced Marshal Ball.

Aspen's breath caught in her throat at the look on Declan's face. He had slipped into his fierce SWAT officer role, and she had no doubt he would never let anything happen to her.

"You and what army? This is more than the local boys in blue can handle."

"You know I'm more than qualified. Me and my men can protect her," Declan snapped. He stalked up to Marshal Ball and glared at him.

"You and your men don't have clearance—"

"You can deputize me," Declan interrupted Ball, who paused. "I'm law enforcement and fit the criteria to be deputized."

Aspen held her breath, wanting what Declan offered, but yet she didn't want to drag him into the middle of this chaos. She wouldn't be able to live with herself if something were to happen to him.

"This isn't something to take lightly, Sergeant. There is paperwork to fill out, and your captain would have to sign off on this."

"He already has. Captain Spook has friends in high places. Just don't take her away tonight."

Aspen stood from her seat, her heart racing. She wiped her sweaty hands on her pants and walked over to Declan. She placed a hand on his arm and stood by him.

"Please. He and his men are good. We wouldn't have to move at all. Between the marshals and the local police, I'll be well protected. I just can't move again," she pleaded.

"One more night, and if this doesn't go through, we are gone."

15

"Thanks." Declan took the duffle bag from Marshal Williams and shut the door. He turned and leaned back against it, hearing the sink run in the en suite bathroom. He swiveled his gaze around the room and took in the queen-size bed, the simple decor of a nightstand and dresser. Thick drapes covered the windows, blocking out the world.

The sound of a click broke through the silence. Aspen appeared in the doorway. She froze and returned his stare. He took in the dark areas beneath her eyes. She looked drained. He was still in disbelief that she was a woman in hiding waiting to testify against one of the most dangerous men in history.

Ray Acosta's rap sheet was longer than a city block. Pride filled his chest that she was going to face a man such as Acosta. It took balls to face someone like him in court.

"Hey," she greeted him. She appeared unsure of herself, almost shy.

"Williams brought you a bag of clothes." He stepped forward and made his way to her. He didn't like the glint of uncertainty in her eyes. He stopped in front of her and held the bag out to her.

She gripped it and held it against her chest.

"Why are you doing this?" she asked.

Confusion lined her face, and Declan wasn't even sure why he was.

She tucked her hair behind her ear and stared up at him. "Believe me, I appreciate you stepping up to try to help protect me, but I can't help but wonder why? We've slept with each other a few times, and I will always cherish our time together. But soon I'll—"

"Aspen, stop." He closed the gap between them.

Panic filled her eyes, and it was escalating in her voice. He tipped her chin up so he could look down into her beautiful eyes.

How did he explain what he didn't understand? "Let me help you, and then we'll figure us out."

"There's an us?" Her voice ended on a squeak.

His lips tipped up in the corner. He wrapped his arms around her and rested his chin on the top of her head. She leaned into him, the duffle bag crushed in between them. He loved the feel of her in his arms and knew he wouldn't be letting her go.

That he knew for sure.

Now the air was cleared, he had a better understanding of why she'd seemed to be hiding something. He ran a hand along her back and knew he'd do anything for her. There was no question that he'd protect her.

Aspen Hale—Irwin—deserved to be able to live her life without having to be hidden or constantly have to look over her shoulder. No matter what happened between them, he would ensure she would survive, testify, and get some form of her life back.

"We'll figure it out." He eased back and laid a small kiss upon her lips. Glancing down at his watch, he saw it was getting close to midnight. "It's getting late. Let's go to bed."

"You're staying here?" she asked, moving to the bed. She sat the bag down and undid the zipper. Pulling it open, she took out some of the items.

"There's no way I'm leaving, Aspen." He moved to the bed and kicked off his shoes. He didn't have any spare clothes with him, and he preferred sleeping naked, but since they were a guest in the home and had two federal agents located in the house, he thought it would be better for him to sleep in his boxer briefs. "That is, unless you don't want me to."

"I want you to stay with me. You make me feel safe," she whispered, holding an oversized shirt.

Her eyes met his, and his stone heart that he had thought would never beat, pulsed.

"Come here." He beckoned her with his finger.

She walked to him with her eyes wide. He had the sudden urge to take care of her. He helped her strip out of her clothes and put the t-shirt on the agent had packed for her.

There was an animalistic need inside his chest to care for her. Even the sight of the shirt on her body made him want to release a growl. It should be *his* shirt covering her, not some random man's. In the back of his mind he was sure it was brand new, but he wanted his to cover her flesh.

He wanted his scent to slide along her body as it brushed against her.

He turned down the covers on the bed and helped her in. Pulling the covers up over her, he tucked her in.

"You aren't getting in with me?" she whispered, rolling on her side. Her hand slid along the bed beside her. Her dark hair flowed over her brown shoulders, creating a dark cloud on the crisp white pillow.

He leaned over and placed a chaste kiss upon her lips. He lingered, loving the feel of her luscious lips.

"It wouldn't be a good idea," he said.

She pouted, and he almost gave in. If he slid beneath the covers and pressed his body against hers, there would be no sleeping.

Damn the feds in the house with them.

"Are you telling me you are afraid to sleep in the same bed as me?"

"I'm afraid there wouldn't be any sleeping." He chuckled then laid another peck on her lips and stood from the bed. He grabbed his cellphone from his jeans. "Get some sleep. We are going to have to get up early."

He stepped into the bathroom and shut the door. Slid his finger against the screen of his phone. Finding the number he was looking for, he hit it and placed the phone to his ear.

"Yeah," a familiar voice answered.

"I need a weapon," Declan stated. No greeting was needed for this call. The gun Aspen had used on the thug had been confiscated for the investigation. If he was going to ensure she remained safe, he'd need a gun.

Aspen glanced down at herself and let loose a groan. The clothes the agent had given her made her look as if she'd enrolled into the Army. Her gray sweatpants had to be rolled up a few times to come above her ankles, and her white t-shirt had Army splashed crossed the chest.

She sighed, wishing for once she could dress as she used to. She would never call herself a snob, but gray

DIRTY BALLISTICS

sweats did not do her ass any justice. She quickly threw the tennis shoes on they had provided her and grabbed her bag. She stepped out of the bedroom in search of the agents and Declan.

She was grateful she had been able to sleep all night. Throughout the night she had sensed Declan in the bed with her, but she guessed he hadn't slept a wink.

"Good morning," she greeted them, finding the men standing around the dining room table.

Declan's gaze dropped to her shirt, and a scowl crossed his face. "Where the hell did that shirt come from?"

"What is that supposed to mean?" Agent Williams asked, crossing his arms in front of his chest.

Declan turned his gaze to the federal agent, and Aspen felt sorry for the agent. Declan's sharp gaze didn't falter.

"A woman such as Aspen deserves quality brands," he announced. His eyes cut to her. "Navy's the way to go."

"Is that so? Army here." Williams turned to face Declan with a smirk. "Navy, huh?"

"SEAL." Declan didn't bat an eyelash returning the stare.

Aspen glanced at Agent Ball, not believing that two men would be arguing over the quality of a t-shirt

143

with the military branch across the front. He rolled his eyes and placed his hands on the table.

"Gentlemen, this is not the time to try to argue the better military branch," Ball snapped, interrupting their stare-off.

Williams settled slightly as Declan walked away and came to her.

"You sleep well?" Declan asked, placing a kiss on her forehead. He glanced down again at her shirt, and the disdain was evident in the look.

She'd have to remember to grab a new shirt when she got the chance.

"What is going on? You guys appeared deep in thought when I came out here," she noted.

"I've been granted special leave to stay with you," Declan said. He reached up and brushed her hair from her face.

"But how?"

"I'll be deputized and then I can be with you the entire time."

"So what does that entail? You take a pledge or something?" she asked, unsure of what it meant. She was thrilled that he'd found a way to remain with her.

"Unfortunately, deputizing someone in the name of the US Marshalls has developed since the Wild West." Ball chuckled. He folded the papers that were on the table before him and straightened to his full height. "We will need to take a trip to the mayor's office to start the process of getting Sergeant Owen deputized. Once he does then he'll be on your case and will assist with your protection detail."

She nodded, already feeling safe.

A knock sounded at the door, and she jumped. Her gaze swept the room. Williams and Ball appeared just as shocked as she felt. They both pulled their weapons out and proceeded over to the door.

Declan pushed her behind him and waited as Ball and Williams ensured they were safe. She peeked from behind him, curious to know what was going on. Ball glanced out the peephole before his body posture relaxed and he lowered his gun. Williams stepped back, away from the door.

"Company of yours?" Ball asked, opening the door.

Declan's friend, Mac, strode through the door with another man at his side. The second man had broad shoulders, a strong jawline, and wavy brown hair. Both Mac and the other cop were dressed in black fatigues. Aspen took in the weapons strapped to their thighs.

Were all the men on his SWAT team built the same?

"Mac." Declan greeted his friend with a strong handshake and manly hug with a pat on the back. He turned to the other man and did the same. "Ashton."

Jesus, what is in the water here in Columbia?

So far, their entire team was large, muscular men who deserved to be on one of those first responder calendars, shirtless.

"What is this, a policeman's reunion?" Ball crossed his arms in front of his chest.

Declan's and his friend's eyes whipped to him, and he seemed to balk under their hard glares.

"Aspen, come here." Declan motioned for her to go to his side. He sent another glare to Agent Ball before turning his attention to her. He rested his arm along her shoulders when she arrived at his side. She leaned into him automatically while he introduced his men. "You've already met Mac, and this here is Ashton Fraser. He's our negotiator and wannabe comedian."

Aspen chuckled watching Ashton dramatically roll his eyes.

"Whatever, man. Hello, Aspen. It's so nice to meet you," Ashton said with a wide grin.

She offered her hand, and he took it, turning it over and laying a small kiss to the back of it.

"Watch it, Ash," Declan growled, squeezing her shoulder. "She's mine."

16

"Do you have it?" Declan had requested a few things when he'd spoken to Mac. He knew his friend would come through with his request. Late-night calls always were answered.

"Everything you asked for is in this here bag," Ashton said, handing him a black duffle.

"And the other thing?"

"Right here." Mac passed him the manila envelope.

Sitting the bag on the floor, Declan took the envelope and opened it, peeking inside. He turned and walked to Agent Ball and Williams. He handed the papers to him with a smirk on his lips.

"What is this?" Ball demanded. He wearily took the papers, glancing over at Williams first.

"Something to speed along the process of getting me deputized," Declan boasted. He didn't have time to waste while waiting on the feds to go through their bureaucratic nonsense. He didn't trust anyone else with the safety of Aspen besides his men.

The room grew silent as Ball read the papers. His gaze flew across the pages while Declan folded his arms over his chest and waited. He patiently watched Ball's eyes flicker to him before handing the papers to Williams.

"What are these?" Williams muttered. He snatched the papers from Ball and read them, too. He paused and glared at Declan. "Where did you get this from?"

"What's going on, Declan?" Aspen moved to his side, concern etched on her face.

"Let's just say we pulled some strings. It would have taken way too long for Agent Ball and Williams to get clearance to deputize me. So I called Mac, and he called our old Navy commander who just so happens to play golf with the Chief of the Special Deputation Unit. He's approving me to be deputized."

Aspens eyes grew wide at the announcement.

"And if you read the fine print, Declan has been granted full federal authority. Meaning he has authority now in any US location," Mac declared. Mac despised the feds and wasn't hiding it.

"Excuse me if I don't believe—"

"Go ahead and call your superiors." Mac's voice

slashed through the air, cutting Ball off. His deep baritone voice was commanding and condescending at the same time.

Declan held back a smirk. He glanced behind him and found Mac's hard gaze on the feds while Ashton leaned against the wall looking calm and collected.

"We will. You have to forgive me. This is not the standard procedure. We must follow protocols—"

"We get it." Ashton sighed dramatically. "Call them. Confirm what you've read on the paper."

Ball's lips pressed tightly in a firm line before he motioned for Williams to follow him. Declan watched them walk down the hallway with their cell phones in their hands. Once they disappeared from sight, he turned back to Mac and Ashton.

"I appreciate you coming." He nodded to both of them. It meant a lot to him that he could call on his brothers and knew they'd be there without asking a question.

"You don't have to thank me," Mac muttered. He moved from where he stood and strode over to the living room window.

"You know the whole team has your back. One word, and the whole team is here," Ashton said.

Declan glanced down at Aspen, seeing confusion lining her face. "Are you all right?"

"I'm just confused at what is going on." She shook her head and let loose a sigh. She stepped away from him and flopped down on the sofa. "I just want this to be over. I'm tired of hiding. I'm tired of having to be protected. I just want my life back."

Declan moved to her and took a seat on the coffee table in front of her, resting his hands on her knees. She turned her sad eyes to him, and his heart lurched. He gently rubbed her soft skin with a small smile on his lips.

"What you are doing is brave." He'd given Mac a little background on what was going on and he was sure Mac had filled Ashton in before they'd arrived. "Just think of all the people who were affected by Ray Acosta. He hurt so many with his greed. You testifying will bring him to justice."

She blew out a deep breath and gazed up at the ceiling. "That's the thing that keeps me going. How could he do it? I've known him practically my entire life. Considered him an uncle, and not only did he murder a man in cold blood in front of me, but he stole money from not just my father's company but all the employees' retirement funds. Some of them were devastated by him."

It pained him to hear the quiver in her voice. Her chest rose rapidly as she tried to regain composure of herself. She lowered her gaze to his, and he was proud at the strength that radiated from her eyes.

"How well do you know those agents?" he asked, keeping his voice low.

Her eyes widened, and she swallowed nervously. "Well, they've been keeping me safe since I was taken from my home and put in witness protection." She glanced around the room before focusing on him. "Agent Ball is the one I deal with the most. He was the one who chose this location and was trying to help me have as normal a life while in hiding as possible."

Declan nodded then sat back. "And the other one?"

"He comes and goes. When he's around I know it's time for me to be moved." She tucked her hair behind her ear.

Declan watched the tremor in her hands.

She was nervous and scared.

"Why did you have to move last time?" Ashton asked. "If you were hidden well, you could have stayed in one place until you were needed back in Cali."

"Umm...the last town I was in was located in Texas. I was at a diner, and the news came on about the case. I was taught that if someone says I look familiar or asks me if I'm Aspen Irwin, I have to report it to Agent Ball."

"You were recognized?" Declan asked. He couldn't begin to imagine what she was going through.

"Not in so many words. But it was too close, and they made the decision to move me here." She looked around the room with a shake of her head. "Moving is getting old. I thought Columbia was going to be the final spot until I testified. I have to take the stand."

"We're going to make sure you get on that stand," Mac growled.

"Damn straight," Ashton agreed.

She turned her attention to them and blew out a deep breath. Her lips turned into a small smile.

"Thank you," she whispered.

"You're welcome, baby," Declan murmured, his eyes locked on hers.

"I do have a question," Ashton announced.

Declan turned and glanced over his shoulder at him.

"Are you seriously okay with your woman wearing an Army t-shirt?"

The marshals returned from the back with grim expressions. Declan stood from his perch on the table and placed his body between her and the feds. She stood and moved so she could see Ball. She knew the look on his face. The pit of her stomach fell out.

It was time to go.

"It would seem that you all have been correct in that my superiors have given me the authority to deputize you, Sergeant Owen. I shall do so, only on one condition."

"What is that?" Declan growled.

Out of the corner of her eyes, Aspen watched Declan clench his fist. She stepped closer to him and gripped his arm in hers. She slid her hand along his forearm and entwined her fingers with his. He glanced down at her and seemed to relax under her touch.

"You stay out of our way and let us handle any threats to Ms. Hale," Ball demanded.

"You sonofa—

"He will," she cut Declan off and held him tight.

He was strung taut, and she was afraid he'd attack. It would be the last thing she need—the feds and local boys in blue fighting in small quarters. From the look of the feds, they were hoping he'd attack. "You won't have to worry about Declan."

"You sure won't," Mac's hard voice cut through the air.

Aspen swiveled her head in his direction and swallowed hard. The cold glint in Mac's eyes had her wanting to step back. If he flew across the room, there'd be no way she'd be able to stop him.

"Settle down, gentleman. There is a lady in the room." Ashton's deep drawl was more pronounced. He pushed off the wall he'd been leaning against and sauntered over to the feds. He purposely put himself between Declan and the feds. "We all want what is best for Aspen. Dec here won't risk her safety."

Declan wrapped his arm around her possessively. She leaned her head against his chest and felt safe in his arms. His chest rumbled as he ran a hand along his face.

"Whatever I have to do, I will. Aspen is important to me."

Her breath caught in her throat, and she looked up to meet his stormy eyes. She swallowed hard and knew he spoke the truth.

"Good, because we have other news." Williams looked around the room. He slid his hands into his pockets and turned to Aspen. "We leave tonight."

"Tonight?" Aspen exclaimed. "If we have the help of the cops here, why do I have to leave?"

She wasn't ready to leave. She wouldn't get to say goodbye to anyone. It was happening again. She'd just disappear and lose everything once more.

She'd miss her job at the library.

She'd miss the only friend she'd made in Columbia

—Evie. She was sure her friend was freaking out because Aspen hadn't reported to work.

"The attack was too close. It's time we move. According to our superiors, you have to return to California," Ball announced.

Declan's grip tightened on her as the room grew quiet.

"Then if that's the case, we'll be happy to give you an escort to the airport," Mac said. It wasn't an offer.

Even Aspen got the message loud and clear. He and his men would be ready to protect her.

All because of Declan. This was the safest she'd felt—ever. Declan's men weren't even hesitating at helping her. She was amazed by his men. They didn't even know her but were willing to protect her.

It made her feel as if she belonged.

And now she had to go face the one man who'd torn her life apart.

She squeezed her eyes tight, the memories of that night coming back to her. Her heart raced with the thought of sitting in a courtroom with that monster.

This was what she had been waiting for. She drew in a deep breath and knew she had to do this. She couldn't let him walk.

It was time to face him.

"Okay, lover boy. Let's get this over with." Ball walked over to Declan, who released her.

She refused to leave his side. He was going above and beyond for her, and she would never be able to pay him back. Her heart swelled with the possibility of what could be driving him to do this for her.

Their eyes met for a brief second, and in that instant she knew she had fallen for Declan.

Once she testified, how would she ever be able to leave him?

17

"You don't think this is a bit much?" Aspen's wide eyes stared up at him.

He smirked and adjusted the ballistics vest on her chest.

"These saves lives," he muttered, securing it around her. He didn't even want to think of her getting shot, much less taking a bullet.

Mac had brought an extra vest for her transport.

Tonight, SWAT would not hunt.

They'd protect.

His men would escort them to the airport to ensure they safely arrived. Declan wasn't taking any chances if the thugs tried to show up again. There was no way he would let them take her.

Mac and Ashton were speaking quietly in the corner of the living room while the feds stood in the kitchen. Declan strained to hear their conversation but was unable to.

"Have you ever been shot before?" Aspen's voice broke through his train of thought.

His gaze turned to her, finding her waiting patiently. Curiosity burned in her eyes, but there was a hesitation, as if she didn't really want to know the answer to her question.

"Yeah." He paused his hands and nodded, flashbacks of the last time a slug hit his vest springing to mind. The damn thing had him black and blue for a few weeks. He had felt fine at the hospital and complained the entire time that he was fine. The next day, he was barely able to get out of bed, for the pain had intensified by then. "It hurt like a son of a bitch."

"Did the bullet go through the vest?" she asked, her eyes growing wider.

He tipped her chin up to him. Her lips parted slightly, and he wished he could claim them like he wanted to.

Not now.

"No bullet will touch you. This vest is a guarantee that we get you there safely. I protect what's mine." His voice ended on a growl. He didn't care who heard him, he wanted it to be known that Aspen Hale—Irwin— was his woman.

Bad guys didn't fight fair, and he'd be damned if they killed her in order to protect a known criminal.

Mac and Ashton's conversation ceased. They'd

heard him. No doubt about it. He glanced their way and found their eyes narrowed on him and Aspen.

"We're ready to transport. Flight has been arranged." Agent Ball stepped into the room. His gaze swept the area before settling on Aspen. "Young lady, in a few hours you'll be meeting with the prosecutor. Hopefully this will all end soon."

Declan moved to the table and finished aligning his body with his weapons. They'd spent the day holed up in the house waiting for night to fall. A calming sensation overcame him. He was used to this feeling. It was the same as if he was going out on a call.

He'd asked for a gun.

Mac outfitted him with enough weapons and ammunition to supply a small army.

"We leave now, we should be at the airport in less than forty-five minutes," Mac murmured, stopping near Declan.

Ashton appeared on his other side. The three of them were dressed in black fatigues. Both Ashton and Mac were decked out in their array of weapons also.

Declan grabbed his favorite weapon, a Glock. The smooth, hard steel was comforting. Holding the weapon was soothing. Declan wasn't sure why, but his gut was screaming something was off.

He glanced over to find Aspen engaged in a conversation with the feds.

"What's wrong?" Ashton's voice was low. He folded his arms across his chest.

"I don't like this," Declan replied, securing the Glock in his side holster. Taking his smaller pistol from the table, he braced his foot on the wooden surface to strap the smaller gun to his ankle. "Why the sudden time change?"

Mac's gaze zipped over to the feds before coming back to him. "Yeah, I didn't like it either."

"To give the feds the benefit of the doubt, they have been working with her for longer. Maybe they are wanting to be unpredictable to throw off whoever is after her." Ashton shrugged, clearly trying to appear casual, but his eyes gave away that he had his doubts, too.

"The plan still on?" Declan asked, glancing back over his shoulder.

"Sure is," Mac confirmed.

"It's time," Agent Ball announced, walking their way.

Aspen came to him and reached for his hand.

His heart leaped.

She was putting on a brave front, but Declan saw the fear in her eyes.

"You're staying by my side." He pulled her close.

Without a word, she jerked her head up and down.

They left the house and filed into a dark SUV. Mac

and Ashton would follow behind in their own truck. Declan knew they would trail the fed's vehicle. Agent Williams closed the door behind Aspen before walking around the truck and hopping into the driver's seat. Declan reached over and yanked her seat belt across her body and clicked it in place.

"I could have done that." Her chuckle was strained, hinting at her stress.

"Humor me." Not caring the agents were in the front seats, he gripped her neck and pressed a hard kiss to her lips. They pulled apart, and he knew he had succeeded in releasing some of her tension.

"All right, lover boy. Time to head to the airport," Ball drawled, climbing in the passenger seat.

The truck started with a gentle purr before it rocked slightly and drove around the semicircle driveway.

Declan turned and watched the headlights from Mac and Ashton's truck flash behind them. He settled back, and Aspen's small hand slid onto his. He turned and entwined their fingers. She squeezed his tight. Their eyes met in the dark, and he returned the gesture.

Aspen's nerves were settled by the feel of Declan's

large, powerful hand holding hers. Her heart raced with the thought of the dangers that awaited her. Going back to California was dangerous, but it was something she'd have to do. There was no way she'd allow Ray to walk. There were too many people depending on her, and she refused to let them down.

The ride was tense, but Aspen would expect everyone to be on high alert after the attack at the zoo. Ray's men knew where she was, and the feds and Declan were taking extra precautions to ensure she remained safe.

She stared out the window watching the wooded scenery fly by. It was late, and there wasn't any traffic on the road. The dark highway road eventually morphed into a quiet suburban area of town. She had driven through the area a few times and recognized landmarks.

Visions of *that* night came to mind.

"California is beautiful this time of year," she whispered, closing her eyes briefly. If she focused hard enough, she could imagine the sunny weather and the winding roads near the ocean. She wasn't sure if Declan heard her, but she had to talk about something to clear her head. She'd replayed that night in her mind a million times, and for once, she had to push it away from her.

"I'm sure it is," Declan rumbled.

"I miss it," she admitted. She turned toward Declan. The darkness surrounded them. Only passing streetlights provided glimpses of his silhouette. The intensity of his gaze slid across her skin. She swallowed hard, not sure if she'd be able to go through with her plan.

Aspen had been planning her own disappearance. After she testified, she'd decided to run. Even if she gave evidence and Ray was put away for life, there were others associated with him who would come after her. She'd learned much about her uncle after being thrust into protective custody.

Her world had been rocked when she was informed Ray was deeply involved in mob life. The money he'd laundered was to pay off debts he owed, and he'd grown greedy and bold. Her findings ruined everything for him.

As a forensic accountant, it was her job to find money hidden. She had been the best. There wasn't a place someone could try to hide money that she couldn't find.

That also meant she was the best at hiding her own money.

There was no way she'd let the feds take her and thrust her into a Godforsaken area of the country to live out her life in fear and poverty.

Once she got the chance, Aspen would disappear.

She planned to leave the country. She'd never be safe here.

Never did she think she'd meet Declan.

Never would she have imagined she'd fall head over heels in love so quickly.

Never would she have imagined she'd have to leave the love of her life.

Again, Ray was taking everything from her. Aspen's heart was tearing in two. She didn't know how Declan would take it, but yet, she wouldn't be around to see the destruction her leaving would cause.

Without saying it, she knew he was in love with her.

No matter how much he had insisted he wasn't the committing kind, his presence beside her in the federal vehicle proved otherwise.

And she was going to shatter the heart he'd given to her.

"Aspen."

She blinked and found Declan looking at her with concern on his face.

"Are you all right? I seemed to have lost you for a second." His large hand brushed her hair from her face. It rested on her cheek.

She leaned into it, basking in the feel of him.

"I'm sorry. I was thinking of something." She sniffed, trying to make up an excuse. It wasn't lying, but she dare not tell him the truth of where her thoughts were going.

A vibrating noise caught her attention. Declan reached into his cargo pants and pulled his cell phone from his pocket. He swiped the screen and read the text message. His cursed filled the air. In the shadows, she watched his eyes narrow on the device before staring up at her.

"What is it?" she asked, an overwhelming feeling of dread filling her.

"We've got a problem." Then he announced, "Ray Acosta escaped from prison."

"What?" she cried out. Her hands trembled with the news. Her mind raced with possibilities. She couldn't go back to California. What if he—

"Williams, you took a wrong turn," Ball snapped, his voice breaking through her rapid thoughts.

Gazing out the window, she saw they were now in an industrial part of town, and from the look of the building, her dread morphed into stark fear. The streets were lined with garbage, and there were plenty of shadows from busted streetlights.

"What the fuck is going on?" Declan growled. His body grew tense, flying forward.

"There's been a slight change in plans," Williams snarled, whipping the truck around a corner, tossing her against the door.

Aspen gasped seeing the glint of a gun in Williams' hand.

"You are no longer needed."

The truck slammed to a halt, and the sound of a gunshot filled the air.

18

Agent Ball's body slumped in the seat. A scream pierced the air, and it wasn't until she shut her mouth that she realized it was coming from her.

"Wouldn't do that if I were you." Williams turned the gun on Declan who froze in place.

Aspen's eyes flew back and forth between Williams and Ball's still body. Her vision blurred from the tears.

"Hands where I can see them."

"Why?" she cried out, holding her hands up. She could sense the rage brimming from Declan. She moved her gaze back to Agent Ball and bit her lip to keep a whimper from escaping.

"Because you are worth a lot of money." Williams' sinister chuckle sent a chill down her spine.

"I'm supposed to be dead. A dead woman isn't worth anything," she retorted.

"Let's just say there's a bounty out on your head,"

he bragged. His gun didn't waver. "And you are worth a lot of money to Ray Acosta—dead."

Declan's growl vibrated through the air. His movement was quick. He flew across the cab of the truck. Aspen gasped, unlocking her seat belt. She turned, not sure what to do. The two men wrestled for the gun with Declan overpowering the agent. Aspen released a scream as they exchanged punches in the compact space.

She glanced around trying to find something that she could use to help. Her gaze landed on William's seat belt. He hadn't put it on. Curses filled the air while the men grappled for the weapon. She yanked the belt and wrapped it around an unsuspecting Williams and pulled back on it.

He let loose a yelp, while she tugged on it, cutting off his air supply. Declan took advantage and slammed his fist into Williams multiple times until his body slumped in the seat.

"What are you doing?" he roared, turning to her.

"Helping!" she cried.

"Out the truck. Now," he snapped. He opened his door and jumped out of the vehicle.

She took his hand and let him pull her toward the edge of the seat.

"I'm sorry, but I wanted to—"

Her words were cut off by the sound of popping.

"Back in the car!" Declan dove inside with a curse, covering her with his body.

Aspen panicked, holding on to him for dear life.

"That's gunfire! Stay down."

Then she heard the pings of bullets hitting their truck. It was coming from both sides. The spray of bullets grew louder. The truck rocked, bullets slamming into the tires.

"Where the fuck is Mac?" Declan tightened his grip on her.

Tears formed with the thought that this was how she'd die. With the way her life had turned out, she had envisioned her death in many ways, but dying in a shootout had not been one of her many visions.

The sound of tires screeching came from off in the distance. More gunfire echoed, and she sent up a prayer that they'd make it out of this situation—alive and unarmed.

Her breath caught in her throat as silence permeated the air.

Sharp voices could be heard from outside.

Declan shifted his body and glanced down at her. "Stay here."

"Don't leave me." She gripped him to her. There was no way he was walking out into that gunfire. She couldn't lose him.

Not now.

"I'm just looking." He shifted his body and quickly glanced out the window. "It's about fucking time."

The door flew open, and her body tensed.

"Someone need rescuing?" a deep voice asked.

"You're an ass, Iker," Declan slid out of the truck.

"We don't have time for sentiment. Those men have big guns and they will be back."

Aspen sat up wearily and glanced at Williams. His body was riddled with holes, and blood was everywhere. Her body shook with the realization that these people seriously wanted her dead at all costs.

"Don't look, baby." Declan turned her head toward him.

She met his gaze and put her trust fully into him. She knew he'd never let anything happen to her.

"Just stare into my eyes."

She jerked her head in a nod. Tears threatened to erupt, but she bit her lip and held them back. Now wasn't the time to burst out crying. She had to hold her shit together and survive. He guided her out of the car and pressed her against him.

"Declan," she whispered. She wanted to tell him exactly how she felt. If she were to die tonight, she didn't want to do it without telling him how she felt.

He must have seen the look on her face because he shook his head.

"Not now. Tell me later."

"Dec," a commanding voice said, the owner stalking toward them with other men decked out in dark fatigues.

Marcas.

Declan brought her close to him. She eyed the men carrying their rifles and guns. They were a fierce group, and she pitied whoever would try to go against them.

"Where the fuck were you?" Declan demanded.

Aspen gasped, his hand tightening on her hip.

"We got lost with the few turns, and Iker was able to catch up to us," Mac responded.

His presence immediately commanded respect, and Aspen could see why he was in charge.

"We need to move."

Aspen glanced around at the men of Declan's team and finally got her answer.

Yes, all the men of Columbia's SWAT team were tall, built, and handsome, but there was only one member of the team who made her heart race.

Declan pulled his gun from his holster and turned to her.

"You don't leave my side. Whatever I say, you do. Got it?" He gripped her cheek in his hand.

Their eyes connected, and she jerked her head in a nod.

"Grab on to the hook of my pants and don't let go."

The sound of a bullet whizzing by and slamming into

the truck behind had her jumping. Declan and his men instantly went on alert. They surrounded her and aimed their weapons at the air, returning fire. Aspen couldn't tell where the bullet had come from, but she moved closer to Declan and grabbed on to his pants as he'd instructed.

"SWAT, let's roll." Mac's voice was cold and deadly.

They moved past the truck, and she tried to keep from looking inside it. She was saddened by the fact that Ball was dead. She didn't have an ounce of pity for Williams. He had planned to turn her over to Ray.

As far as she was concerned, he'd got what he deserved.

"We need to take cover," Mac directed. "Ash and Zain pulled back. We are to meet them over on Pine Street, a block over."

The team was like a well-oiled machine in their movements.

One block.

His team was the best. They'd make it.

Only this time, they had an extra person with them.

Aspen.

He hadn't thought twice about covering Aspen's body with his when the bullets began raining down on them. He was proud of how strong she had been. Anyone else would have lost their shit, being in a car being riddled with bullets.

Not Aspen.

She'd held on strong.

When he'd pulled her from the truck, the look in her eyes was enough to almost bring him to his knees. He'd known what she was about to say at that moment, but it wasn't the right time.

Declan would ensure they had time to sit down and talk about this thing between them.

He wanted more.

He wanted her.

She was the one for him.

They may have sped from zero to a hundred, but he didn't care. Their entire relationship had been unconventional.

After this mess, they'd have forever to get to know each other and plan a future.

Declan held back his curse and knew he had to focus on her security. That would be the only way they'd be able to have a future.

Once the gunfire ceased, he'd never been so glad to see his brothers in blue. Brodie, Myles, Mac, and Iker had been a sight for sore eyes. When they got out of this mess, he'd owe them all cold beers.

But right now, he had to get his woman to safety.

Aspen's tight grip on his pants comforted him and allowed him to keep both hands free.

He fell behind Mac as they ran toward the closest building. Myles and Brodie flanked Aspen's side while Iker pulled up the rear.

The dilapidated building was abandoned. The street Williams had brought them down was the perfect place for an ambush.

"Where are they coming from?" Brodie snapped.

The sound of random bullets hitting the pavement littered the air behind them as they made it to the building. They pressed close to it.

Declan put his body in front of Aspen's, looked around sharply, but under the cover of night, it made it almost impossible. He didn't like this one bit. Dread rested in the pit of his stomach, and he always trusted his gut.

Something was off.

Myles and Iker hid behind two wide columns and knelt on the ground. Both of them had flipped their visors down over their eyes, giving them sight into the pitch-dark night. Their weapons were trained toward the building across the street.

"Rooftop. Tango thirteen hundred," Myles

murmured, his rifle steady. He was the team's lead sniper. Once Myles locked on a target, it was good as dead.

"Got it," Iker responded.

"We need to keep moving," Declan snapped.

Gunfire echoed again, but this time a single shot silenced the enemy fire.

"Got him," Myles announced. "There were a few more up there with the him."

"You guys go. We'll cover and fall behind," Iker threw over his shoulder.

"Stay close." Declan turned to Aspen.

She jerked her head in a nod. Her grip on his pants had yet to falter. Her face was lined with fear, but she didn't complain.

Mac moved along, his weapon trained high. Declan followed behind with Brodie waiting for them to pass, and he now brought up the rear. He gripped his Glock tight, keeping it raised and his finger on the trigger.

They came upon a set of glass doors. Mac paused, hoisting his fist in the air.

"We're going through the building," Mac rumbled. "It's abandoned but dark."

"Are you fucking kidding me?" Declan cursed. Pure darkness could mean anything.

"It's either take our chances in here or get shot out

there. There's no telling how many are on the rooftops." Mac glared at him.

Declan didn't hesitate to return the heated stare.

Brodie stalked past to the edge of the building and peered around it. "The alley isn't better. We'd be sitting ducks."

"I don't like this," Declan said. It was one thing for them to enter a building on jobs, but now they had an innocent civilian with them. "Stay here, Aspen." He pressed her against the brick wall and undid her firm grip on his pants.

He moved near the door and glanced through the glass. It was dark, but he was able to see the doors on the other side. Lights from the neighboring street filtered through the door.

That would be their target destination.

Five hundred feet of the unknown.

He glared back at Mac who was waiting on him.

"Through the building or around it?" Mac cocked an eyebrow.

"My vote is through the building," Brodie said, coming to stand beside Mac.

The exchange of gunfire sounded behind them.

Cursing floated from where Iker and Myles were.

Declan turned back to the front and aimed his gun at the edge of the glass and fired. The crackle of glass shattering echoed through the tense air. Grabbing Aspen's hand, he pulled her next to him.

"Stay behind me," he ordered. He wasn't taking any chances. If any were hidden in the building, he'd rather take a bullet than her. Now they knew Ray was out of prison, he was a man who truly had nothing to lose. "Don't look anywhere else but straight. We are going to make a run for it through this."

You are worth a lot of money to Ray Acosta—dead.

A rage unlike any he'd ever felt crept into his chest at the thought that someone Aspen had trusted had betrayed her.

He would not lose Aspen.

Not now.

Not when he'd finally found the one who made his heart beat, who filled his every waking thought.

Iker and Myles arrived at his side.

Mac turned to them all, his face stone.

"Let's move."

19

Aspen's body trembled with fear. She'd be damned if she acted like a scared female. She put her complete faith in Declan and his men. There was no other way she'd survive if she didn't. They entered the building silently. Declan placed a finger to his lips to signify for her to remain quiet.

You don't have to tell me twice.

Even if she wanted to say something, she was gripped by fear that her throat wouldn't allow any sound to pass.

How does he do this every day?

She certainly had a better perspective of the men of SWAT. They bravely put their lives on the line so people like her could remain safe.

The men moved quietly. She strained to hear anything, trying to use her senses in the low light. She placed her hand out and rested it on Declan's ballistics vest. The feel of it comforted her. Hers was tightly encasing her body.

At the time Declan had placed it on her, she'd thought it had been overkill.

Now look at her.

Being hunted down.

Her breaths were coming fast as they crept through the building. Her eyes adjusted, and she could see the open plan. There were no walls. Only open space and large support pillars lining each side of the warehouse. It was stripped down to nothing but stone and rubble.

"Straight ahead," Declan whispered.

She snapped her eyes back forward and focused on the SWAT stamp on his back.

Tension filled the air while they pressed on.

Halfway there.

She almost forgot to breathe. Mac and Brodie kept their rifles raised, sweeping the area. The other two, Myles and Iker, silently trailed behind them. They had fanned out around Aspen while Declan led the group.

A sound of metal rattling echoed. Aspen jumped. A squeal escaped her lips before she could clamp her hand across her mouth. The men focused their attention over to a dark corner. Brodie clicked on a flashlight, and Aspen blew out a deep sigh of relief.

The debris on the floor in the corner rolled away, revealing a fat rat scurrying along the wall.

"Keep moving," Mac's low voice jerked them all back into motion.

Aspen kept her gaze ahead. The SWAT team was more protection that she'd ever thought she'd need, and right now she was grateful to them all.

They neared the doors. Aspen let out an unsteady breath. She watched in amazement as the men communicated with hand signals. Mac directed Brodie and Iker to the door.

Declan reached behind and drew her closer to his back. She molded to him, comforted by his strong presence. She gripped his arm tight, feeling the tension rolling off him in waves.

"I see the trucks," Iker whispered.

His words were music to Aspen's ears. Declan kept his hand on her and lowered his gun. He stepped forward, aligning them behind Brodie.

Mac moved to Iker's side, and she watched, amazed how Declan and Mac communicated without saying a word.

One look and a nod.

They truly worked together as a team.

"Keep your head down. I'll guide you to the first truck," Declan instructed her.

Her heart slammed with the thought of stepping back out there. The sounds of the bullets hitting their truck reverberated in her mind. Fear gripped her, but she was able to nod.

"You can do this. We won't let anything happen to you."

"Got it," she managed to choke out. Heart pounding, she took a deep breath.

Declan turned away from her and motioned with his hand.

Brodie stood and stepped back from the door. "I'm going to have to shoot the lock," he announced in a low voice.

Declan turned and put his body in front of her, pushing them away from the door. He wrapped her in his strong embrace. She closed her eyes and breathed in deeply again. Her body jerked from the sounds of the two soft pops.

"Clear," someone said.

Declan pulled back, and his fierce gaze comforted her. He turned and gripped her arm. Myles disappeared through the open door first with Iker and Brodie in tow.

"You two first, then I'll follow," Mac instructed.

Declan nodded and led her toward the door. The streetlights allowed her to see the two identical trucks idling in the middle of the street.

Her heart seemed to lodge itself in her throat as

they stepped outside. She took in the sight of Declan's men posted in the street with their guns raised. An eerie feeling passed through her, chilling her to the bone.

She locked her gaze on her target.

The trucks.

"Let's go. Don't let go of my hand, and keep your head down," Declan growled.

Declan tightened his grip on Aspen and tugged her away from the building. He cursed, wishing the trucks could have gotten closer. The area behind the dilapidated building gave off the look of a post-apocalyptic area. Trash and debris lined the road with abandoned cars and dumpsters. The buildings across the street were in the same horrible condition, practically crumbling before his eyes.

This would be the longest dash ever. He wouldn't have worried if it was just him.

His gut was screaming for them to run to the car, but his training kicked in, and he assessed the area they were about to walk into.

Bad guys could be posted anywhere.

His team was spread out, covering them. His Glock in his hand brought him some comfort, but he'd have to admit he wouldn't be settled until he could get Aspen to safety.

The events in the truck with the federal agent turning on them had him in a rage. Had he not pushed to accompany Aspen, there would be no telling what would have happened to her.

Something whipped through the air and slammed into the building behind them, grabbing Declan's attention.

"Shooter!" Iker's voice sliced through the tense air.

Another bullet slammed into the hood of Ash's truck.

"Get her in the truck now!" Mac hollered, firing his gun in the direction the shot had come from.

Aspen's scream pierced his ears as they backed up against the building again.

Then came the sounds of motorcycles flying down the street toward them.

What the fuck?

"Let's go!" Declan grabbed her hand, practically dragging her behind him toward the second truck.

Zain's fierce gaze met his as they grew closer.

Bullets began raining down on them.

The motherfuckers were on the rooftop across the street.

His team returned fire, providing cover.

Three men on the bikes wore dark clothing, helmets, and drove their dirt bikes closer.

Brodie turned, firing at the bikes. His bullet tunneled into the first rider, throwing him off his machine.

Declan gripped Aspen's hand in his while raising his gun. He fired, hitting the second rider whose bike flipped over.

Aspen screamed, and her hand slipped from his. As if in a nightmare, Declan watched her body jerk before she fell to the ground.

"Aspen!" he hollered, not recognizing the sound of his yell. He glanced up.

A shooter hung out of a window from the building they'd just got out of.

"Myles!" He aimed his weapon and pulled the trigger once. He released a curse, watching his bullet slam into the brick building, missing the intended target.

Myles ran to his side and aimed his weapon at the building.

He knelt by Aspen's side. Her wide eyes were full of pain. Seeing the pool of blood underneath her, he released a curse. Her body writhed on the ground in agony as she gripped her leg.

"Come on, baby," he murmured and scooped her up in his arms.

She cried out and wrapped her arms around his neck. He took off in a dead sprint toward the truck where Zain had been waiting. The back door flew open, allowing him to crawl inside with her.

The sound of her cry broke his heart as he shut the door behind him. The passenger door flew open with Brodie jumping inside.

"Let's move!" Zain yelled out of his window.

The sound of wheels screeching filled the air above Aspen's pained cries. The truck jerked as Zain made a hard turn and flew away from the trap. Declan's eyes were fixed on Aspen, trying to find where she'd been shot.

"Declan," she gasped.

"Where are you hit?" He roamed his hands over her legs and came away drenched in her blood.

Their bodies tilted as Zain took a hard turn.

He'd watched a bullet slam into her vest and had felt his heart leap into his throat. If he could find the fucker who'd dared to shoot her, he'd kill the man with his bare hands.

"My leg," she moaned when he grazed his hand along it again, trying to find the wound.

His hand met the soaked area of her jeans. A curse slipped from his lips.

Her front thigh.

"I've got to put pressure on it," he murmured,

pressing down on it. She screamed and writhed on the back seat. "We need a hospital!"

"We've got company," Zain growled.

Declan glanced up and met Zain's eyes in the rearview mirror. Declan was confident in Zain's ability to handle the road. It was engrained in all of them.

The back window shattered, spraying glass everywhere. Declan ducked, leaning over Aspen.

"Stay with me, baby," he pleaded.

Her pain-filled eyes met his, and she jerked her head in a nod.

"Hold us steady!" Brodie shouted, rolling his window down as another truck sped up beside them.

Declan sat up. Brodie expertly shot out the tire of the truck which sent it careening off the side of the road. It slammed into a pole.

Zain controlled their truck and drove off, flying like bats out of Hell.

Declan glanced down and found Aspen's eyes closed.

"Aspen!" he shouted over the roar of the engine.

She didn't respond. His heart pounded as he shook her. He tightened his hold on her leg. Her head rolled to the side, and a fear like he'd never known gripped him. He released her leg and reached for her neck, trying to find a pulse. "No, no, no, no."

"Call ahead to the hospital and let them know we're coming with a gunshot," Zain snapped to Brodie.

He navigated the truck through the streets.

Brodie's voice faded to the background.

"Aspen, stay with me. Don't leave me," his voice cracked.

His whole world was crashing down around him. He was supposed to protect the one person who gave him a hope for a future, and he'd failed.

20

Declan closed his eyes and leaned forward, resting his head in his hands. He blew out a deep breath, unable to get the image of an unresponsive Aspen out of his head. He sat in the empty waiting room, replaying the sight of her being shot in his head. He released a growl, blaming himself for not taking better care of her.

He would gladly have taken a bullet for her.

In the truck, he'd practically wept with joy when his fingers finally found her thready pulse. They arrived at the Emergency Room with a team of medical professionals meeting them at the door with a stretcher. They'd swept her away from him, leaving him to stand in the doorway of the hospital with an empty feeling in his chest.

"Are you holding up?" Mac appeared near him.

Declan opened his eyes. Black boots stood in front of him. Glancing up, he found his team standing before him.

He'd lost track of time and didn't know how long he'd been sitting in the waiting area. They hadn't allowed him to find out any information on Aspen. The only things he'd been told was that she was alive and was in surgery.

So he'd flopped down in the chair, refusing to leave.

"They won't tell me anything," he growled, standing.

Zain, Brodie, Ashton, and Iker stood silently behind Mac.

"Don't worry. Sarena is working on that." Mac reached out and gripped his shoulder.

Mac's fiancée was an assistant nurse manager of the Emergency Room. He felt somewhat relieved by the fact Sarena was going to help him.

He rested his hands on his hips, and his team settled into chairs around him.

"You guys don't have to stay. You've done enough—"

"We're not leaving," Ashton announced. He settled back in his chair with a defiant look on his face.

"I don't have any place to be at for the moment," Zain said, folding his muscular arms in front of his chest.

Declan ran a weary hand through his hair and

looked around at his men. They each dared him to try to send them away.

"Look, I really—"

"Stop," Mac snapped, cutting him off. He ran a hand along his face and waved to their team. "You know we protect our own. The minute she's out of surgery, there will be someone on her around the clock. I know your stubborn ass won't let her out of your sight, so we're going to be here to help."

Declan jerked his head in a nod, his throat constricting.

"She's one of us," Iker said. He leaned forward, resting his arms on his knees. It had been Iker keeping him from tearing the head off of one of the doctors when they'd barred him from Aspen's room.

The doors of the waiting room burst open with Myles striding through them. The look on his face was grim, and the men to stood from their chairs.

"Declan." Myles nodded to him. "Mac. I just got off the phone with the captain. The feds and local boys in blue are all over that fucking alley."

"Do we know who any of those fuckers are?" Brodie asked.

"Not yet. I'm sure we'll know soon," Myles replied.

"That was a lot of man power. Someone with deep pockets definitely wants your girl dead," Ashton said.

The room grew silent, and Declan agreed.

"My federal contact had notified me that Ray Acosta had escaped from jail. There is a nationwide manhunt for him. I had just texted Dec when all hell broke loose," Iker announced.

Curses filled the room with the news.

Ray Acosta may have just escaped from prison, and still somehow he was able to send a small militia after Aspen. It was even more imperative that Declan be able to protect her. A man like Ray was going to be desperate and wouldn't quit until he got what he wanted.

Aspen dead.

"Federal agents are on their way here now and will be assuming protective detail," Myles said.

"How the hell did they know where we are?" Mac scowled.

The tension in the air grew tense as they all waited for a reply.

"Someone called it in to the feds. They are on their way to the hospital now." Myles shrugged before shoving his phone in his cargo pant pockets.

Declan bit back a curse. With all that'd been happening with Aspen, he'd been distracted from his attempt to find out the leak in the department. Whoever notified the feds had to be the same person.

"The leak," Brodie snapped, running his hand through his hair. "We've got to find the leak."

"The feds would have found out eventually when they didn't show up at the airport," Iker cut in.

Everyone paused, knowing what he said was the truth.

"How do we even know it was from our department? It could have been any of the men who were working with that fucker, Williams," Zain spoke up. "There's no telling how many crooked feds are involved."

"Right now, it doesn't even matter. We know what's going to happen when the feds show up," Mac's voice slashed out.

"They aren't keeping me from her," Declan stated. He narrowed his eyes on his friend. Even being deputized for this assignment wouldn't keep them from taking her.

"Mac," a soft voice called out.

Declan swiveled his gaze to the door and found Sarena standing there. Dressed in her scrubs, she stepped into the room. Mac stalked across and took his fiancée in his arms for a hug.

"Sarena." Declan made his way over with the rest of the guys in tow. Nerves filled his gut as he waited for news of Aspen.

She pulled back away from Mac, and Declan approached.

"Dec." She brushed her hair behind her ear and

stared up at him. "She pulled through surgery. They're moving her to a private room in the Intensive Care Unit. I've spoken with the manager of that unit, and they will allow you to see her, but only during visitation hours. So you'll be able to see her in a few hours."

Relief flooded him at the news. He nodded, taking the small victory.

"The only thing is..." She paused, glancing around at the lot of them.

"What is it, babe?" Mac asked gently.

It always amazed Declan at the difference in Mac when he was around Sarena. It was as if she truly was his other half. He was calmer and less of an ass when with her.

"The hospital has already been notified that she is to be guarded. They are putting her in the isolation room to keep traffic away from the main part of the unit. They don't want other patients' care to be compromised by having guards around. There's federal agents everywhere down there."

Declan's stomach gave way at the news. He turned and brushed past Zain to take in a few breaths, ignoring his name being called.

His mind raced at the thought that the feds would keep him from her. Rage festered and built in his chest. A red haze clouded his eyes. He braced his hands against the nearest wall, trying to breathe. He felt the walls closing around him.

He was suffocating.

Aspen was his.

He needed her, like he needed that next breath.

Ray Acosta would not get his hands on her. If he'd escaped from jail, there was only one thing that would be on his mind.

Finding Aspen.

Declan knew how they worked. The feds would swoop in and take her, uncaring if she were injured or not. They just wanted her for their case. They didn't really care about her. If they did, they would have known their man had gone rogue.

His breaths were coming faster, and the anger built up in him and exploded.

Letting loose a yell, he slammed his fist into the wall. Shouts filled the air.

She belonged to him.

He slammed his fist into the wall again, ignoring the pain.

Thick, muscular arms wrapped themselves around him, pulling him back from the wall. His fist pulsed with pain. He didn't care. He'd rather take the pain of a broken hand than experience the pain of losing Aspen. If they took her, he would never see her again.

"Aspen!" he yelled.

Curses sounded as he was taken down to the floor. He fought them, swinging his fist. Satisfaction surged into him as it connected with something.

"Dec! Get ahold of yourself," Mac's familiar voice snapped in his ear.

A knee was pushed deeper into his back while his arms were clamped down by two bodies.

"I have to get to Aspen," he gasped, unable to move beneath the massive weight pushing him to the floor.

"Not like this. Get your shit together," Mac said. "She's going to need you, but I swear to God, if you don't get it together, I will have you locked up."

The fight left Declan. He relaxed his body and rested his head on the floor. Mac was right.

He couldn't lose his shit right now.

His woman needed him.

"Are you good?" Iker asked, his voice a level above a growl.

Declan blew out a deep breath and nodded. "I'm good." He closed his eyes and allowed the images of their night at the safe house to fill his mind. He'd held her in his arms while she slept. Her face had been relaxed and utterly beautiful. He'd held her close the entire night, barely sleeping a wink.

He wanted that again.

To hold her in his arms and never let go.

Aspen breathed in deeply and immediately regretted it. Her lungs burned like fire, and her throat felt as if someone had sliced it with razor blades. Her body was overcome with coughing, but a piercing pain in her legs made her cry out.

"Oh God," she whispered, opening her eyes.

A bright light blinded her. She raised her hand to shield her eyes to allow them to adjust. She glanced around at her surroundings and found herself in a hospital room. A standard hospital gown covered her body. She was tucked away in a bed with rails up the sides. She moved her body as much as she could, wincing from pain. "Declan?"

Her heart raced with the thought of being alone. She swallowed hard and winced from the pain. She licked her parched lips, finding them dry and chapped.

She took in the room. Curtains lined it. The walls were glass, but the curtains provided privacy for her. A man sat with his back to the her outside the door.

He must be a guard.

But where was Declan?

The sounds of beeping had her turning and looking at the monitor that displayed her vitals. Memories of running from the building and the feel of the bullets slamming into her back crowded into her mind. She could still feel the white-hot burning sensation in her leg.

Oh God. She'd been shot!

Her heart rate was increasing right before her eyes with the memory of Declan picking her up and running to the car.

Seventy-three.

Eighty.

Ninety.

The door slid open, revealing a nurse walking through it.

"Oh good. You're awake," the nurse said with a gentle smile.

Her smooth, brown skin was flawless. Her dark eyes held a curious note, but she didn't ask the questions that were smoldering in her eyes. Her dark hair was pulled up in a bun, and her scrubs were dark but didn't hide her curves.

Aspen didn't say a word but watched the pretty woman walk over to her machines that were on a pole delivering intravenous fluids into the tubes connected to her. She eyed the tape on her arm and felt the cool fluid entering her veins.

"Where am I?" Aspen asked. She grimaced hearing her voice sounding like nails on a chalkboard.

"You're in intensive care. You underwent surgery to get that bullet out of your thigh." The woman paused and stepped closer to the bed. Her eyes were gentle as she studied Aspen. "I'm Ronnie, by the way."

"I'm Aspen," she whispered. She winced at the pain it took to talk.

"Here, let me help you. The doctors ordered this soothing spray for your throat. It's probably sore from when you were intubated during the surgery." Ronnie turned and grabbed a bottle with red liquid in it.

Aspen read the label with a familiar name on it. She opened her mouth, and Ronnie sprayed a few squirts inside. The cooling spray instantly calmed the scorched sensation in her throat.

"If that leg of yours hurts too much, hit this button, and pain medication will be dispensed to you to help keep it under control." Ronnie lifted a small device with a red button on the tip.

"Thank you." Aspen tried to smile, but her cracked lips prevented her. She took it from Ronnie and hit the button. A beep sounded from the machine it was connected to.

"Don't need to thank me. I'm friends with Sarena. You've met her before, right?"

Aspen nodded, thinking back to the day she and Declan had lunch with Mac and Sarena. It seemed like eons ago.

"She told me to pass along that Declan is here. But you're under heavy guard now, and they won't let anyone who isn't a federal agent or hospital staff into your room. I was able to bribe the other nurse to switch patients with me so I could have you." She patted Aspen's hand with a smile.

Aspen felt somewhat comforted knowing that if Declan couldn't be here right now, they'd at least found a way to send a friendly person to be with her.

"Thank you." Aspen couldn't help but say it again. "What happened?"

"You took a couple shots to the back. Thank God you were wearing that bulletproof vest. You are going to be sore for a while. But the real issue was your leg. You took a bullet in your thigh, and it lodged itself into your femur. Had it been an inch or two higher, it would have hit your femoral artery, and I don't even want to say what could have happened if that would have been the case."

Aspen gulped with that knowledge. She wasn't medically trained, but hearing a bullet hitting any artery didn't sound good.

"I don't even want to know what could have happened." Aspen shook her head.

"You were in good hands. The surgeons were able to dig it out without causing too much damage. Now you relax. I'm going to let Dr. Murphy know you are awake. He's one of the surgeons who operated on you." Ronnie backed away from the bed and turned. She disappeared out the door, leaving Aspen alone once again.

She settled back against the pillows, feeling the effects of the pain medication kick in. Her body relaxed, and her eyes drifted shut.

21

Aspen felt herself being pulled from her dream. The physicians had come with Ronnie and examined her, pleased with the sight of the wound. Her leg still burned, and she was assured that it would feel better by the next day. The surgeon had ordered a scan to be performed in the morning to ensure there was no internal bleeding since the area was hot to touch.

Since then, she'd floated in and out of sleep. The pain medication made her drowsy, but it took some of the edge off.

Dreams of Declan threatened to pull her back under, but something was off. Her body swayed, and she realized her bed was moving.

Her eyes flew open, and the sight of the ceiling rolled past.

Panic filled her chest, and she glanced up. A man in dark scrubs with a mask covering his face pushed her bed. The cool air brushed her face as he sped up.

"Where are you taking me?" she grumbled, trying to shake the fog from her brain.

Was it morning already? She didn't think she'd slept that hard or long.

"Shut up," he snapped.

Well, that certainly wasn't the way to speak to a patient.

She looked at him and frowned. Fear crept into her chest with the thought of where he was actually taking her.

She may have been a little loopy from the medication but she was no dummy.

He is not hospital personnel.

She frantically took in her surroundings and found herself being pushed down an unfamiliar hallway. From what she could tell, it looked as if they were in the basement of the hospital. Strangely enough, there wasn't anyone around for her to call out for help.

"They are going to be looking for me," she warned. She didn't have much to threaten with. Hell, she didn't even know if they'd realized she was gone yet. "The feds and the police—"

"I said shut up, bitch," he snarled. "Or I'll shut your mouth permanently."

Her lips snapped shut. The pain in her leg was throbbing, and she needed to push her pain button. She glanced up and saw her IV pole still attached to her bed, but there was no way in hell she was going to take the happy drugs and drift off to her wonderfully drugged sleep at a time like this. She'd just have to grin and bear it.

They turned a corner, and the perfectly esthetic hallway turned into what looked to be a large storage facility. Her gaze landed on large loading dock doorways, and she finally understood where they were.

The underbelly of the hospital.

Late at night, the maintenance employees weren't around, and deliveries would not be happening at this time.

Her heart skipped a beat as a few men stepped from behind large pillars. One familiar figure stood apart from the goons and captivated her attention.

The one person she'd hoped to never see on this side of a set of prison bars stood not twenty feet from her with a scowl embedded on his face.

"I knew you weren't dead," Ray sneered.

"And I just knew you'd be in prison forever," she remarked. She took in a deep breath and refused to show fear. There was no way she'd let him know how frightened she was.

His dry chuckle met her ears. She glanced around and took in five men with him. Each of them were armed with weapons visible on their bodies. She stared at Ray and saw the man she'd grown up with and thought of as an uncle, but the man whose murderous gaze met hers wasn't that same person.

"You're still a smart-ass." He shook his head. "Come here, Aspen."

Her eyes widened, thinking of the pain she was in lying down. She didn't even want to think of the agony she'd be in taking her first step.

"I don't know if you know, but I just had surgery to remove a bullet your man put in my leg," she snapped. How the hell was she supposed to walk?

"Well, you're lucky he only hit your leg. Too bad. He should have been aiming at the middle of your forehead." Ray nodded to the man who had pushed her down.

The masked man came alongside her bed and snatched the IV line from her arm. She cried out from the sting of the tape and tubing being removed.

"You're not going to get away with this," she gasped as the man dragged her to the edge of the bed.

He wasn't gentle at all. Her vision blurred with tears. The pain in her leg exploded, and she cried out. Her back was sore and ached as if she'd been hit with a bat. She didn't even want to imagine what it would have felt like if she hadn't worn the vest.

"But I will. Do you know how much I had to spend to find you? How many agents I had to bribe?"

"How could you do this to us?" she screamed. She

batted the masked man's hands from her. She wasn't going anywhere with Ray. If they took her, she knew she'd never see Declan again. She'd watched with her own eyes, Ray take a man's life. What was stopping him from doing the same to her? "You were like an uncle to me. I looked up to you." Her voice ended on a hitch.

Ray stalked toward her and stopped directly in front of her. "You left me no choice, Aspen," he snapped. He settled his hands on his hips and waved his thug away. Ray returned his attention to her with a look of disgust on his face.

This was not the man she'd grown up with. No longer was he the man whose pool she'd swum in as a child. No longer was he the proud uncle who had attended her high school and college graduations.

That person was long gone.

Instead, a cold, hard killer stared at her.

Her body trembled from the force of the pain rushing through her. She swayed for a second, her body threatening to fall over. She fought to stay sitting up, not wanting to appear weak.

"You had plenty of choices," she whispered. Tears slid down her face, and she no longer cared. If he was going to kill her, he might as well do it now. She would fight to the death before she let him take her from the hospital. "My father trusted you."

"Your father was an idiot. I had big plans, and he just shot them down. I was ready to take our business to the next level."

"Well, it looks like you have a little more pressing matter at hand. Breaking out of jail won't help your case—"

"You don't worry about me, Aspen. I won't be standing trial," Ray cut her off. "You think you are the only one who is good at hiding money?"

Her quick intake of breath had a chuckle spilling from his lips. His eyes narrowed on her.

"What are you talking about?" Her voice was just a decibel over a whisper. Her mind raced. She had been careful over the years. What she'd stashed had taken years for her to accumulate. It had always been her rainy day fund. She always believed that one should save money in offshore accounts.

Just in case.

"Oh, don't try to play dumb, Aspen. I know you are extremely intelligent. It took me a while, but I finally found proof that you have been putting money away—"

"There's no crime in that," she snapped. Her leg throbbed, and her breathing rate increased. She was beginning to feel light-headed and knew she was going to be in trouble.

"Doesn't matter. You're going to give that money to me."

"I am not!" she exclaimed, shaking her head. "You're trying to tell me that you have nothing? No money?"

"They stripped everything from me!" he screamed. He paced the floor.

The thugs shifted uncomfortably around the room as they watched him.

"Talk about a system that brags about the 'innocent until proven guilty' theory. I haven't even got to trial yet and they've already convicted me. All of my bank accounts have been frozen. Even my offshore accounts can't be accessed. But yours, they will be mine. Because of you—"

"Me?" she shrieked. The bastard couldn't believe everything that had happened to him was her fault? "This is all your doing!"

"And I'm going to fix it," he taunted, pausing before her.

Ray snapped his fingers, and she watched with dread—one of his men approached. He was tall and solid muscle. His dark skin was roughened with scars above his right eye and one on his lower lip. His beard was thick, and his eyes were black as midnight. She swallowed hard as he pulled his gun from his holster.

"This is not a request. You are going to transfer the money to me. I'm leaving this fucking country, and you are going to be my ticket out of here so I can disappear."

"Why, so then you'll kill me afterwards?"

"Kill you?" Ray scoffed. "You're already dead."

A fear like she'd never known gripped her. She was trapped between a rock and hard place. Either she refused and they killed her now, or she give him what he wanted and she died later. Either way, she didn't see him allowing her to remain alive much longer.

"Now stand," Ray ordered.

Her gaze swept the large room, and she sent up a prayer that Declan and his men would swoop in and save her.

Aspen swallowed hard. She blinked a few times before scooting to the edge of the bed. Her bare toes touched the floor while fire shot up her leg. She bit back a whimper, not wanting to show her pain. Ray's man turned his gun on her, and she had no other choice but to stand. Putting her weight on her good leg didn't help once she was on her feet.

Her body shook, and a warm substance trailed down her leg. Her body swayed, and the room darkened.

Ray released a curse, and she lost her fight with consciousness and slipped into a dark abyss.

22

"Excuse me. When I can I visit Aspen Hale?" Declan asked the woman behind the nurses' station.

Her eyes widened when she looked up and met his. He was on a short fuse. They'd kept Aspen from him long enough. Mac had been on the phone with the captain trying to get clearance for him to visit with her.

It was bullshit that he couldn't go see her. He'd been on her detail before the plans had gone to Hell in a hand basket.

"I'm sorry, sir. We are not allowed to let visitors in to see her." She smiled apologetically. "It's not our rule, but the agents told us unless you are a federal agent then we can't allow anyone in her room."

"When did this change? I was told I would be able to see her during visiting hours?" he demanded to know. But he already knew the answers. Now the feds were here—they would run the show.

He lowered his gaze to her badge and read her name.

Susan.

"Susan, do you have loved ones?" His voice dropped low. He narrowed his gaze on her, his temper rising. He gripped the counter, trying to remain in control and not lose his shit. He didn't care that she didn't make the rules.

She visibly swallowed hard and nodded. Her eyes widened with tears forming.

He ignored them.

"What if the one person who mattered to you was lying in a hospital bed, alone, scared, and you were unable to be with them. How would that make you feel?"

Guilt.

He wasn't above using it to get what he wanted.

"Umm..." She swallowed hard again, wiping a tear that escaped down her cheek. Her fair skin paled. She wiped another tear that slipped from her eye again. "Sir, there's nothing I can do—"

His attention was caught by the sight of people rushing by down the unit behind her. He pushed off from the counter and walked to the edge of it, curious as to why they'd be running. The nursing staff was in a full-blown panic.

"Susan." A nurse rushed up to the secretary. Her eyes were wide and frantic.

Declan recognized her as the nurse who had relieved Ronnie. It had been time for Sarena's friend to get off, and she'd left to go home to get some sleep with the promise to return in the morning.

Declan's stomach dropped.

Something was wrong.

"What is it, Megan?" Susan turned to the nurse.

Declan wasn't hiding the fact he was openly listening to their conversation.

"We need to call security and a code yellow," Megan announced.

"What the hell is a code yellow?" Declan snapped.

Susan snatched her desk phone up and began speaking softly into it.

"Internal emergency. Missing person. My patient, Aspen Hale, is missing—"

Declan didn't wait to hear any more. He dashed around the desk, ignoring the nurse yelling after him. He instantly took off toward Aspen's room. He only knew it was hers because of the thick crowd standing in the doorway.

Pushing through the people, he saw the agent assigned to watch Aspen on the floor with a pool of blood beneath his head. His skin was pale, and he appeared lifeless.

Doctors and nurses were hovering over him, working on him, but Declan's attention was drawn to the empty spot where Aspen's bed should have been.

She was gone.

Declan's heart slammed against his chest.

Where the fuck was she?

"Code yellow," the operator's voice burst through the hospital overhead intercom system. "Code yellow. Intensive Care Unit. African-American female. Five feet—"

Declan brushed past the people and exited the room. He turned and found Mac and his team stalking toward him. People in the unit automatically cleared the hallway at the sight of the pissed-off cops. They were all still dressed in their black fatigues, their badges dangling from around their necks, and they each were armed, their weapons strapped to their waists.

The Columbia SWAT team was a formidable team and wasn't to be taken lightly.

"What the hell happened?" Mac barked.

"I don't know. Her entire bed is gone, and the agent is being worked on by the doctors." Declan ran a trembling hand through his hair. He gave a quick recount of what he'd seen in the room.

"Whoever took her can't be far," Ash said, folding his arms across his chest.

"Shouldn't there be other security here?" Iker asked, looking around the nursing unit.

"Who the hell knows." Declan shook his head. There should have been. Aspen was a high-profile witness, and there should have been more.

He should have been at her side.

Visions of Aspen's wide grin came to mind. He was flooded with images of her naked brown skin against his and her beneath him. The feel of her plump lips pressing against his when he kissed her still haunted him.

He needed her and he'd be damned if someone would take her.

He turned to Mac who placed a strong hand on his shoulder as if reading his thoughts. Mac understood what he was going through. It wasn't too long ago they were in each other's shoes.

"We'll find her," Mac assured him. He squeezed Declan's shoulder before turning to the sound of people rushing toward them.

The hospital security had arrived.

Declan took one look at the group and glanced at Zain who cocked his eyebrow in disbelief.

This was security?

Four members of the hospital security team, in identical uniforms of light-blue button-down shirt and dark pants, came strolling through the nursing unit.

They were led by an aging, overweight man who appeared as if he gave up on taking care of himself years ago. The other members consisted of a kid who barely looked as though he'd reached puberty, a middle-aged black woman whose glasses perched on the tip of her nose, and a tall, lanky man who seemed like he'd rather be anywhere else than in the hospital.

"You boys sure do show up fast. I'm Bob Smyth," the older man announced, stopping in front of them.

Mac stepped forward and shook the man's hand.

"I'm Sergeant MacArthur from Columbia SWAT. We just happened to be here and we're willing to help," Mac said.

Declan knew he'd used the word 'help', but what he really meant was that they would take the lead. This band of security guards would be no match for the men who'd taken Aspen.

Gathered in the hospital's emergency command center, they made plans of how to find Aspen. Thanks to the hospital security cameras, the entire scene of Aspen's kidnapping had been recorded. The sight of her being taken fueled his rage. Declan went through the motions of preparing himself for this search-and-recovery.

This time, it was personal for him.

The situation had been called in to the station. Mac had spoken to the captain and notified him of the situation, and their team was officially activated. With them already at the hospital, their gear was brought to them from the station. Each member of the SWAT team was suited up and ready.

Declan gripped his MP5 and slapped his helmet on. He was ready to go after Aspen.

I'm coming, baby.

They had watched the CCTV videos a few times, and the scenes were permanently engrained in his memory. The guard, now admitted to the hospital, was seen being taken by surprise. The hallway had been cleared when a man with a surgical mask in place to hide his face, dressed in scrubs, walked behind him. The man hit the unsuspecting guard in the back of the head with his weapon, rendering him unconscious. He dragged the agent into Aspen's room and shut the door. What happened in the room, they were unable to see, but Declan had been a witness to the aftermath.

Declan watched in stark horror, a sedated Aspen being wheeled from her room and down the hallway without anyone questioning where the masked man was taking her.

The kidnapper literally strolled out of the unit

pushing Aspen, and not one person realized the man was not a hospital employee.

"We're going to need a hospital emergency team on standby." Mac's voice pulled Declan from his thoughts. Mac, as always, was in charge of the SWAT team and barking orders to everyone who was going to be a part of this rescue.

"We'll be ready. The Emergency Room is ready, and we even have an operating room freed, just in case it will be needed," a physician answered.

A team of highly trained medical individuals stood off to the side, waiting.

Since the news had broken in the hospital that they not only had a missing patient but a potential hostage situation, it had gone on lockdown.

"And you have evacuated everyone from that area?" Mac asked, turning to Bob.

Declan would have to give the hospital security team credit for allowing the police force to take control of the situation. This was not a normal occurrence of an unruly patient or family member they were used to dealing with.

No.

Men like this were much more dangerous.

They were killers.

"Where he took her is what we call the catacombs. It's the underworking belly of the hospital. Shipping and receiving is down there, and the boiler rooms." Bob brought out the blueprints of the basement. He spread them out on the table before them. "Right now, their only exit out of the hospital without coming back up to the main floor would be through the delivery doors."

"Squad cars are down there now, blocking them. They are trapped," Iker announced, disconnecting a call on his cell phone.

"Any other exit they can use besides the shipping docks?" Declan asked. His gaze roamed the blueprints, and he memorized the area where Aspen was being held.

"Yes. The catacombs run along the hospital. They could come out this side and be near the Pine Street entrance." Bob's finger slid along the prints and tapped an exit point. "There's a staircase that leads to an emergency exit."

"We'll need to have that exit covered—" Mac was interrupted by Ashton.

"Mac, we have a problem. The feds are outside." Ashton pulled his phone away from his ear and let loose a curse. "They are demanding to speak to the officer in charge."

Mac's gaze flew to Declan, and he already knew what Mac was thinking. Mac didn't have the best relationship with the feds. He and a federal agent had clashed when it came to the SWAT team rescuing

Sarena during her ordeal. It would be best if that agent never showed his face again in Columbia.

"Who is asking?" Declan asked. He already knew he was on a short circuit and wouldn't be the best person to act as liaison between SWAT and the feds either.

"Someone named Agent Turner." Ashton shrugged.

"Fine. But he better not get in our way." Mac turned back to the blueprints with the team surrounding him.

Ashton began quietly speaking into his phone.

"We'll enter from the shipping dock. It will give us more room, and we'll not be in a funnel trying to enter from the basement. We don't have time for negotiations. We're going in hot."

Declan was focused on the prints and had officially memorized them.

"Hey! We got video down there. The cameras picked up on men down in the shipping dock," one of the hospital security guards announced. He brought over a laptop and set it down beside the blueprints.

"Show me," Declan demanded, moving next to the guard.

His team crowded around him with Mac standing next to him. The guard tapped a few commands on the computer and brought up the video. Declan's stomach clenched when he saw exactly who had his woman.

Ray Acosta.

"How the hell did he make it all the way from a California prison to here? There's been a countrywide manhunt for him?" Ashton asked.

"Who the hell knows. Better question is: how did he know Aspen was alive?" Iker responded.

Murmurs went around at his words.

How the hell did Ray know she'd still be alive?

"Is this live?" Declan asked, trying to pinpoint a timeline from the moment she'd disappeared. He didn't like what he saw on the video. Aspen looked vulnerable lying in the bed.

There was no doubt in Declan's mind that Ray would want Aspen dead. She was the one person who could send him away to prison for the rest of his life. She was a loose end that he'd need to tie up. At least if there was a slight delay, from what he could tell from the video, she was still alive.

I'm coming for you, baby. The words echoed in his head, and he wished there was a way for Aspen to hear him.

He gripped his MP5 tight, comforted by the fact they were going to go after his woman.

He'd shoot his way through anyone who tried to stand in his path.

Aspen Hale was his.

"SWAT," Mac's voice broke through his thoughts.

He narrowed his eyes on his close friend. Each team member stood at attention. There was a gleam in each of their eyes that relayed they were ready for this. Mac was a fierce leader, and Declan trusted him with not only his life, but Aspen's. Declan was certain they would return with his prize.

"Time to hunt."

23

"Ray, you told us this would be a simple snatch and grab," a voice snarled, breaking through Aspen's pain-filled fog.

A groan slipped past her parted lips while she fought to open her eyes. Confused, she opened her eyes and took in her surroundings. Her gaze roamed the area, and she found herself in what looked like a loading dock. She shifted her body, and a sharp pain zipped through her. Her hand shot out and immediately went to her thigh, but the pulsating pain wouldn't allow her to touch it.

She cried out, clenching her eyes shut, letting out a deep breath. Her eyes fluttered open, and her attention landed on the figures standing next to her, deep in an argument.

Ray Acosta.

Her memories rushed forward.

She had been taken from her hospital room and

was now in the hands of the one man she'd hoped she'd never see again.

"Look, your men were supposed to take care of her twice and failed both times. Don't come bitching to me because you couldn't kill her," Ray snapped.

The other man pulled his gun from his holster. The men surrounding them paused, their gazes locked on them.

"Why don't I just take care of her now?" The man stepped toward her with his gun raised to her head.

She froze in fear, her heart pounding.

"Are you an idiot?" Ray snapped.

Aspen couldn't take her eyes off the gun. There had been so many things she'd wanted to say to her family, her friends, and Declan. Facing death again, she knew that if she ever got to speak to any of her loved ones, she would not let a day go by without telling them how much they meant to her and how much she loved them.

Her eyes widened, knowing deep in her heart that she loved Declan. The relationship between them had been quick and unconventional, but he was the one for her.

Without a doubt in her mind, she knew it to be true.

And staring into the barrel of the gun, she didn't see herself ever being able to tell him.

"The hospital is on lockdown, and she's going to be our ticket out of here." Ray stepped forward, clearly unafraid of the man. The gun wavered before lowering to the ground.

Tears slipped from Aspen's eyes before she knew it. Her heart raced, fearing the unknown.

"Well, since you're so smart, you better get us out of here," the man demanded, putting his weapon back in his holster.

The men surrounding them appeared to relax, but Aspen didn't trust any of them.

Ray turned to her, and her breath caught in her throat.

"Welcome back," Ray said. He walked over and stopped at the edge of her bed. "Thought we'd lost you for a second."

"I need help, Ray," she said, her voice cracking. She felt weak, and the pain was excruciating while her breaths were short and getting harder to take in. "Turn yourself in. Let me get help."

"And go back to jail?" He snorted. "That won't happen. Now let's try this again. Get up."

He raised a gun and pointed to her. Her vision blurred. She blinked the tears away. With a sigh, she bit her lip and slipped toward the edge of the bed.

"I'm no good to you if I die, Ray," she whispered.

"I just need you to transfer that money to me, and then you can die for all I care." He smirked.

"There's cops outside," the bearded man snapped from his position by the door. He moved away from it and stalked toward Ray.

"Don't worry." Ray waved a hand at the men. He turned toward Aspen with a sinister grin. "We all know how the police will work. They'll call us and try to bargain with us. Once they do, we'll play the hostage card and demand—"

The lights went out, casting them into darkness. Curses went around the room. The tension palpable before was now suffocating.

Aspen couldn't see anything in front of her face, much less where Ray or any of the men were. The sounds of glass breaking filled the air. Even in the dark, Aspen could tell the men were scrambling around the room.

"They're going to call and bargain with us, eh?" a man shouted.

"Let's go, Aspen," Ray snapped.

A firm hand gripped her arm and dragged her to the edge of the bed. She was surprised by the strength of the older man. He must have benefited from the gym while in prison.

If she wasn't in so much pain, she'd roll her eyes.

This time, he forced her up on her feet. She cried out and fell into his body.

There was no way she'd be able to walk.

"Just leave me," she begged, gripping his shirt in her hand to try to hold on to him.

"Not a chance." He wrapped an arm around her waist and hauled her along next to him.

Something pressed into her side, and she instantly knew what it was without needing to see it.

A gun.

"I'm going to slow you down. I can't even walk," she cried out.

"Shut up!" he hollered, digging the barrel of the gun deeper.

The sound of pounding thudded, and Aspen's heart jumped. Wood splintering met her ears, and it was a noise she'd never thought she'd be glad to hear.

"CPD!" a deep voice shouted. "Freeze!"

Ray turned around and brought her body up in front of him. Tears streamed down her cheeks. The pain rippling through her body was unbearable. Her breaths were coming fast while her body trembled uncontrollably.

She jumped at the bang of a gun firing. Return fire could be heard with shouting. Men cried out in agony, followed by the sounds of bodies crumpling to the floor.

Aspen fought to stay conscious. There was no way she could afford to pass out now.

"Don't shoot! I have the girl!" Ray shouted.

She whimpered as the gun was pressed farther into her side.

"And turn the damn lights on! I'm sure you wouldn't want me accidentally shooting her."

"Aspen?" a familiar voice called out.

Relief swamped her at the sound of Declan, rage suppressed in his voice. There was no doubt in her mind that he was pissed off.

"I'm here," she replied, hating how weak she sounded.

"Are you injured?"

"That's enough!" Ray cut them off. "Now I want to make my demands known."

"You don't get any demands," a voice growled.

Aspen recognized that voice as well. It sounded just as pissed off as Declan's had.

Mac.

"Really? I'm sure you'd think different after I put a bullet into Aspen," Ray threatened. "She's my ticket out of here."

"Putting a bullet in her will ensure you'll leave here in a body bag," Declan snapped. "Your choice, Ray. Walk out of here in cuffs or wheel out of here with a fucking tag around your toe."

Ray remained silent. Aspen held her breath. The lights flashed on, temporary blinding her while she squinted to allow her eyes to adjust. Ray's grip tightened around her waist. He moved the gun and placed the barrel at her temple.

Aspen opened her eyes fully and took in the room before them. Each of the men who had sided with Ray was laid out on the floor, writhing around in pain. A few were on their stomachs with their hands tied behind them. But what caught her eye was the sight of the SWAT team in their black fatigues with their weapons trained on them. Some of the men were kneeling near the other thugs on the floor while others stood with their murderous gazes trained on Ray.

One figure stood out. One she was intimately familiar with. She'd never seen a more beautiful sight in her life.

Declan.

"Think, Ray," another voice spoke. This one was calmer than Declan and Mac.

If she remembered right, it was Ashton, the one who had come to the house with Mac. "We don't want anyone else getting injured. Let's do this in a civilized manner. Hand us the girl so she can get medical attention. We can all walk out of here."

"I'm good as dead returning to prison," Ray yelled. The barrel of the gun pressed harder against her temple. "There is no way I'll be returning to prison. I'll be dead before the doors even shut. She comes with me. You're going to let us—"

"Not an option," Declan growled.

"Then you leave me no choice." Ray barked a sinister laugh. "Her death will be on your hands. This is the last time I'll say it. Let us both go, and you can get her later after she transfers her offshore account money to me so I can disappear forever."

"If it's money you need," Ashton began but was cut off by Ray.

"Let me guess, you will provide it? What, do you think I'm stupid? I know how you cops work. No, Aspen hid enough money to allow me to disappear and live out the rest of my days."

"I'm sure the feds will offer protection," Ashton replied.

The SWAT team shifted, but their guns never wavered.

"We can't let you leave here with the hostage. She needs medical attention now. Let's just get out of here safely together, and we'll work something out."

"The feds? I bought them off and found where Aspen is. That's easy as hell. I'll be found in no time under the protection of the feds," Ray snorted.

He removed the gun from her head, and Aspen closed her eyes, not knowing what to expect.

"There are always other choices."

Aspen braced herself. Time appeared to slow. Shouts could be heard, and the sound of a gun firing barked near her.

Her body jerked from the close fire of Ray's weapon. Ray's hand slid off her body as his crashed to the floor behind her. Without the help of him holding her up, her knees buckled, and she fell to the floor. She groaned, turned over, and glanced back at Ray, finding a pool of blood underneath his head.

Footsteps sounded towards them. She blinked, trying to fight the darkness from reclaiming her.

"Aspen!" Declan flew to her side and rolled her over.

She lost sight of Ray as people surrounded him.

"Baby, are you all right?" he asked. He gripped her chin and brought her face towards him. His eyes, full of worry, gazed down on her. "Aspen. Can you hear me?"

She reached up a shaky hand to his face and cupped his cheek. She closed her eyes and whispered the three words she never thought she'd get to say to him.

"I love you."

Having said them, she allowed the darkness to take her.

24

Declan sat beside Aspen's bed. This time, there was no argument from anyone. He would have fought anyone who would have denied him entrance to her hospital room. It had been close to a week since that dreadful day when he'd thought he'd lost her. The sight of her being held with a gun to her temple had ripped a hole in his heart.

In the end, Ray had taken the coward's way out and shot himself in the head, ending everything.

In his selfishness, little did he know he had set Aspen free.

"My beautiful sleeping Aspen," he murmured. He reached for her hand that was free from the IV tubing and ran his fingers along her smooth brown skin. She had been through so much.

The minute Ray had fallen to the floor, his team had immediately kicked in. They'd secured the room, the other thugs were processed, and the medical team was then able to enter the room to work on Aspen. She had passed out, but not before saying the three words he'd held dear.

I love you, she'd whispered.

The medical team had whisked Aspen away, and she was immediately taken to surgery. Her leg had sustained damage by walking on it. According to the surgeons, she had been bleeding inside the wound, making the leg swell. They'd gone in and released the pressure and cleaned it out. Declan was told she may have a slight limp, but with good physical therapy, she should recover completely.

They just needed her to wake up. The physicians had kept her in a drug-induced coma to give her body time to heal. She'd lost a lot of blood while being held captive. The hospital bed she'd been on down in the shipping area had been drenched with it.

Had Ray not taken his own life, Declan may have assisted him along, seeing how Aspen had been treated. The other men who worked for Ray were currently sitting in jail.

Now she was resting in a private room in the hospital. This time, no intensive care. Just a unit that offered privacy and the best of care.

Right now, staring at her, he knew what he wanted. He wanted to hold her in his arms again and feel her curvy body against his. He wanted to be able to kiss her and let her know that she wouldn't ever have to be scared of anyone else again.

The sight of terror in her eyes had almost brought him to his knees when faced with her being held hostage.

"How is she?"

Declan glanced over at the door and found Mac and Sarena. He waved them in.

"Same." He blew out a frustrated breath. Once she did wake up, they were due for a talk. There was so much on his mind that he didn't even know where to begin. Federal agents had come and gone. They, too, were waiting to speak to Aspen.

"It may take time," Sarena murmured. She stepped at the other side of the bed and offered a small smile.

"That's what the doctors keep saying," he replied. At the moment, he wasn't sure he could even smile. He ran his fingertips along Aspen's arm, willing her to wake up. "I hate to say, I'm just impatient."

"Well, she's been through so much. I'm sure she's just waiting to make her dramatic entrance." Sarena chuckled softly.

"How are you holding up?" Mac asked, cocking an eyebrow. "You look like shit. When was the last time you showered?"

"Marcas!" Sarena gasped. She took a seat on the

windowsill and glared at Mac who promptly ignored her.

They'd been friends long enough for Declan to know Mac was concerned about him.

"I couldn't even tell you." Declan shrugged and ran a hand through his hair.

"If you want, one of us can stay with her to allow you to go shower." Ashton's voice had Declan turning to the doorway.

Ash and Brodie stood in the entrance while Iker, Myles, and Zain were present behind them out in the hallway.

"Yeah. You don't want the first thing Aspen smells when she awakens to be your funk." Brodie chuckled.

Ashton rolled his eyes and gave Brodie a slight shove with his arm.

"Cut it out." Mac glared at their team before turning his attention back to Declan. "They're right, you know."

"We can hold down the fort. I'm sure the hospital has a shower you can borrow. I bought some clothes for you," Myles announced, pushing past Ash and Brodie. He walked over toward Declan and tossed a duffle bag at him.

Declan caught it and stood from the chair. He glanced down at Aspen and gave her hand a slight squeeze.

"Well, if you insist," Declan began.

"We do," Brodie, Iker, and Myles replied simultaneously.

The tension was broken up by chuckles floating around the room.

What would he do without his team? They were as close as brothers, and he wouldn't want to work with any other group of men. They truly looked after one another.

Declan shook his head and leaned down and pressed his lips to Aspen's forehead. Her dark eyes remained closed. Her chest rose and fell in a slow, steady rhythm.

"I'll be back in soon," he murmured.

He straightened and moved away from Aspen. He stood at the foot of the bed and caught the eyes of his team who filed into the room. Iker and Zain found a spot on the floor while Mac sat next to Sarena. Myles took the seat vacated by Declan while Brodie remained near the door.

"Thank—"

"No need." Ash held up his hand, cutting Declan off. Ash leaned back against the wall and shook his head. "Just go. We'll stick around until you come back."

Declan grimaced and ran his hand along his face, feeling the week's worth of a beard filling out on his face. Brushing past his men, he headed down the hallway knowing Aspen would be in good hands until he returned.

Aspen felt herself floating amongst the clouds in her dream. She didn't want to leave the peaceful state. There, she'd been lounging around in Declan's arms. If she didn't know any better, she would have thought it had been real. She'd found safety and solace in his embrace and knew that like in real life, she wanted to stay there forever.

But the vision of Declan vanished before her eyes, leaving her to float aimlessly amongst the white fluffy clouds. Her vision of the serene place began to dissipate, and reality hit her.

She breathed in deeply and blinked. The walls of a hospital room greeted her once again. The sounds of beeping filtered through along with the slight rumbles of snoring. Her gaze went to the IV pump that was placed near her bedside. She tried to move her body and found her leg was just sore. Remembering the pain she'd felt before, she assumed they'd had her on pain medication.

She turned her head to the opposite side of her bed, and her gaze landed on Declan slouched down in the recliner next to her. His dark hair fell over onto his forehead, and she ached to brush it back. In a dark t-shirt and jeans, he slept.

Her lips curled up into a small smile as she took him in. Memories of him rescuing her came to mind, and she froze in place. Tears flooded her eyes, and everything came forward.

The shoot-out.

The hostage situation.

Ray taking his own life.

With him dead, she was free.

A cry tore from her lips, and Declan's eyes flew open.

"Aspen," he gasped, sitting forward. He stood and immediately sat on the bed next to her.

"Declan," she croaked.

He reached over and grabbed a small cup of water and a straw and held it to her lips. She took a few sips to alleviate the aridness from her throat. He put the cup back down on the side table and turned to her. His large hands gently brushed her tears away off her cheeks.

"Welcome back, baby," he murmured.

She gripped his hand and leaned into his touch. She closed her eyes and basked in the feeling of Declan.

"Why the tears?"

"Because it's over with, right?" she asked. Her

heart raced with the thought that she was finally free and would no longer have to be in protective custody.

She could have her life back.

"Yes, it's over. With Ray dead, there is no need for you to testify."

Sobs racked Aspen's body. Declan pulled her to him and enclosed his arms around her. She held on to him tight and let all of the emotions flow out of her. Without saying a word, he just held her and let her cry it out.

She had lost so much, and now with Ray out of the picture, she could finally move on with her life.

She'd lost track of time. She sniffed and knew Declan's shirt was drenched.

"I'm sorry," she whispered.

"What do you have to be sorry for?" Declan asked. He slid a finger underneath her chin and tipped her face forward to meet her eyes. "After everything you've been through, I'd say you needed that."

"But I got your shirt all wet and I think there's snot on it, too," she whined, embarrassed.

"I think I'm built tougher than that, Aspen. I'm here for you, and if you want to cry on my shoulder, I'll take all the tears and snot." He chuckled.

She couldn't help the smile that appeared on her lips. She swatted his shoulder.

"Declan, there's so much I want to say," she began, but was cut off by his finger pressing against her lips.

"Before you say anything, I have something I need to get off my chest," he announced.

Her heart raced with the possibilities of what he was about to tell her. She bit her lip and nodded. He removed his finger and smiled. "Aspen Hale—Irvin—I love you. I know you've been to Hell and back and will need to get your life back in order, but I want you to know that I am in love with you."

"Oh, Declan," she breathed. Tears welled up in her eyes, and this time she brushed them away.

How did she think she'd be able to walk away from him?

"I was talking to the feds, and they are going to restore your life back to the way it was," he began, and this time, it was her turn to put her finger to his lips.

She shook her head. "I don't want my life back to the way it was before all of this craziness."

He stared at her. "You don't?"

"No. If it went back to the way it was before I discovered what Ray had been doing or witnessed him shoot that man, I wouldn't have you in my life. I need you, Declan." Her voice cracked, and he leaned forward and pressed his lips to hers.

"You just don't know how good it feels to hear you say that."

His unwavering gaze held hers, and she could feel herself getting lost in his eyes.

"It's the truth," she admitted.

"I'm not rich, Aspen," he began. His hand cupped her cheek while his thumb slowly stroked her skin. "I'm a retired Navy veteran, living on a policeman's pay."

"None of that matters to me." She smiled gently. It didn't. Even if she'd never saved money in those offshore accounts, she would be happy starting over in life as long as Declan was by her side. "I just need you to love me."

"Always."

25

Declan stood back and watched while Aspen addressed the press alongside the federal prosecutor and federal agents. He couldn't have been prouder of her in that moment. She was dressed in a killer business suit, her hair flowed down her back, and her outfit was completed by the fashionable cane Sarena and Ronnie had gifted her.

He wasn't sure where'd they found a cane with a fake diamond handle and a shaft decked out gold and black, but it fit Aspen's personality perfectly.

The media was having a field day on this story. Once the death of Ray Acosta was released, the media had been in a frenzy. Finding out that Aspen had been placed in protective custody and had not perished in the accident as reported, really had them salivating.

He was sure answering questions over her ordeal was drumming up the bad memories, but Aspen remained cool and collected the entire interview.

"No more questions," Wilson Lloyd, the prosecutor, announced, holding his hand up.

The small crowd groaned, seeing they wouldn't be able to ask anything else. The cops and agents in the room directed the members of the audience to the exit to allow Aspen and Wilson to leave the podium.

Declan's feet carried him over to the stage. He held his hand out to Aspen and assisted her down the few stairs. Over the past weeks, she'd had to work with physical therapists. She'd done exceptionally well with all of her therapy since being released from the hospital. She handled everything with grace and determination.

"You did good, babe." Declan was rewarded with her killer smile, and his heart skipped a beat. He guided her toward the back entrance. "Let's get out of here."

They left the room and began the trek down the hallway of the downtown federal building.

"That was nerve-racking, but I'm glad we did this. It helped close the door to that chapter of my life." She squeezed his hand.

He slowed his stride to allow her to keep up with him. Her limp was still noticeable, but she had been determined to walk unassisted today.

"Miss Hale, before you leave," Wilson called out behind them.

Declan slowed to a halt and turned to see the federal prosecutor making his way to them. He shuffled along, dressed in his tailored suit, his briefcase in hand.

Aspen moved closer to Declan, wrapping her arm around his forearm. He glanced down at her. Her weary gaze met his, and she let loose a sigh.

"I just want to go home," she said, leaning her head against his shoulder.

They'd had a long day dealing with the feds and then the press.

"Miss Hale." Wilson arrived, stopping in front of them.

"I need to get Aspen home. She's tired from this circus," Declan stated. He squared up and faced the prosecutor while sliding his arm around Aspen's shoulders. He didn't have a problem with dismissing Wilson. Aspen had done everything they'd asked of her. Her time of assisting the feds was over.

She wanted to go home.

He'd take her home.

He would always protect her.

"Of course." Wilson nodded. "If there is anything else I can do for you, please let me know."

"Thank you," Aspen replied, leaning into Declan.

"I just want to remind you that restoring someone's life has never been done before—"

"It's okay. I know who I truly am. The new last name and social security number I can get used to. It didn't change me. Ray may have caused me to lose so much, but I do have to thank him for one thing."

She patted Declan on his abdomen, and he squeezed her shoulders.

He had to agree. Had it not been for Ray, she would have never been whisked away to South Carolina.

"Again, if I can be of assistance, please don't hesitate in calling me." He held out his card, and Declan took it.

"Will do." Declan nodded and guided Aspen toward the door without looking to see which way Wilson headed.

He'd parked his car right outside the back entrance of the building so they'd be able to make a quick escape. They quietly exited and made their way to Declan's car. He helped her into the ride before jogging to the driver's side and hopping in.

"Declan." Aspen leaned her head back against the headrest with her attention on him.

He hit the button to start the car and turned to her.

"I love you," she said.

"I love you, too." He smiled. Unable to resist, he leaned over the armrest and laid a kiss on her forehead. "Now let's get you home."

He put the car in drive and pulled off. They remained in a comfortable silence as he navigated the car through the light traffic. Thoughts of the surprise he had waiting for her filled his head, but he couldn't help notice Aspen was being too quiet.

"What's wrong, Aspen?"

"Nothing." She sighed.

"It doesn't sound like it." His gaze darted to her for a second before turning back to the road.

"I was just wondering. You haven't really asked me much about that night Ray had me."

He knew he hadn't. So much had gone on that night, he was just thankful she had survived. But a few things had plagued him, but he figured whenever she was ready to talk about things, she would let him know.

"I didn't think you were ready," he admitted.

"I am. I don't want us to go on with any secrets. If I am to heal completely, I'll need to heal my mind *and* body. So ask me a question." She tossed her cane in the back seat and turned to face him.

He could feel her gaze on him and knew now was the best time to ask her.

"When Ray was screaming about offshore banks. Was what he was saying true?" He guided the car to a stop, pausing at the red light. He glanced her way and met her eyes.

"Yes." She blew out a deep breath. "I'm a forensic

accountant. Do I trust banks and the government completely? No. So a long time ago, I began saving my money in offshore accounts. My family is very well off, and I put some of my money in accounts to build a hefty nest egg."

"And that's what Ray wanted from you?"

"That, and me dead." She nodded.

"If he would have gone to prison, what were your plans?" If Ray had wanted the money in her account and was willing to risk being captured to obtain it, must have meant it was a shitload of cash.

Her lips curved up into a small smile as she tucked her hair behind her ear.

"I had planned to disappear and never come back. There's enough money there for me to live off of for the rest of my life. The world would have been my playground."

His heart stuttered for a moment. Was she still planning to leave? Now that she didn't have to hide who she was, what were her plans? They hadn't really discussed a future. They had been focused on her recovery and rehab.

"And now?" he asked. He held his breath, and the light turned green. A car horn honked behind him, and he focused back on the road and drove.

"I sort of like it here in Columbia. This hot police

officer has my heart, and I don't think he plans on letting it go."

He smiled and winked at her. Relief filled him at her response. "You're damn right I'm not going to let it go."

Aspen gritted her teeth as she slowly made her way up the stairs to Declan's apartment. After being released from the hospital, she didn't want to step foot in her house. She never really cared for the neighborhood, and now that she was free to do what she wanted, she would have to find a place to live.

But she was in no rush. Since being discharged, she'd stayed with Declan, and they'd fallen into a nice routine.

She tried not to think of the ordeal, but it would take some time. Her leg was a constant reminder of getting shot while running for her life. She hated that she'd been in the hospital when US Marshal Ball's funeral was held. He may have been a hard-ass, but he had died while trying to protect her.

"Two more stairs, babe," his voice rumbled behind her, breaking into her thoughts.

"Don't be looking at my ass," she called out over

her shoulder. She giggled at the light touch of his fingers grazing the curve of her backside.

"I can look all I want," he muttered.

She celebrated internally at making it up the last stair. Declan came up behind her, and she waved off his hand. She needed to be able to do this herself. Her handy dandy cane was all she needed for the moment. She was determined to be able to walk free without any assistive device and only wanted to hold Declan's hand because she wanted to, not needed to.

The door to the apartment across the hall swung open.

"Aspen!" Evie flew out of her apartment with her blonde hair in a high ponytail. She collapsed her hands in front of her chest with small smile on her lips. "You did amazing."

"Thanks, Evie." Aspen allowed her friend to wrap her up in a hug.

Evie had at first been shocked and then disappointed that she hadn't known about Declan and Aspen's relationship. Her friend had been at the hospital almost every day after hearing what had happened. It had meant a lot to have Evie at her bedside along with Declan. Between the two of them and Declan's team mates stopping in to check on her, she'd felt as if she'd gained a new family.

"You guys need anything? I'm sure you must be tired. I can run out and grab us a bite to eat—"

Her bubbly attitude was sending Aspen dizzy. She smiled at her friend and shook her head.

"We're good, Evie." Declan raised a hand. He unlocked the apartment door and turned back to them. "We're just going to take it easy today and probably just order pizza."

"Okay. But let me know if you change your mind and want something else. I don't mind running out—"

"We're good, Evie. You've done so much already." Aspen gripped her friend's hand. "Believe me, we'll call if we need something. Right now I just want to take this suit off and get into some relaxing clothes."

"Gotcha." Evie nodded before going back to her door.

Aspen waved and walked toward Declan. She turned back and found Evie watching them with a shit-eating grin on her face. Aspen rolled her eyes and stepped into the apartment. She knew that look. Evie had been gloating ever since finding out that her matchmaking attempt had worked.

Declan shut the door, but Aspen barely heard him come up behind her. She stood frozen in place, unable to believe her eyes.

"Mom? Dad?"

26

"Did you really think we'd not look for you?" Mason Irwin shook his head and patted her on her knee. Aspen had lost track of time since she'd discovered her parents standing in the middle of the living room.

"What do you mean? I read the stories. I saw the news coverage. They were very convincing that I was dead. Hell, if I didn't know any better, I would have assumed I was dead, too." Aspen shook her head.

She was still in shock that her parents were sitting on Declan's couch with her. Declan had stepped into the back room to give them some privacy and make a few phone calls.

"Your father refused to believe them," Donna Irwin whispered.

Aspen's mother's eyes were as red and puffy as Aspen was sure hers were as well.

"But the funeral. I saw videos of it," Aspen said. She had watched that video quite a few times and each time she broke down crying seeing the pain her parents had gone through.

"It had been our decision to have it. Our emotions got the best of us. We knew were truly burying Aspen Irwin. We never thought we'd actually see you again. We'd learned the feds had put you in protective custody and we didn't want to push to see you for fear that Ray would be able to discover you, too."

"Well, he did," she replied quietly. It had been all too easy for him to track her down.

"Well, now that's behind us. We will recover and move on," her father stated.

He rubbed her knee, and a small smile spread across her lips.

Yes, they all would recover. She knew it must have been hard on her father to discover that not only had his best friend betrayed him but he'd also stolen from him and tried to kill his daughter.

It would take time, but they would all persevere.

"That's a fine young man you have there," her mother announced.

Aspen turned to her with wide eyes. "I know. He's come to mean so much to me," she admitted.

"I'm just thankful he was able to save my baby." Mason's eyes grew serious as he gazed into hers. "He's a good man, Aspen. From what I've read on him, he's a keeper."

"Read up on him? Daddy! What did you do?"

"You don't think I wouldn't run a check on the man shacking up with my daughter, did you?" He shrugged and leaned back on the couch.

"Your father means well." Her mother chuckled. "But I agree with your father. Declan certainly seems like he could be the one for you."

"Well, we agreed to take it one day at a time—"

"For what? You know the story of us. Our courtship was a whirlwind." Her mother's eyes grew dreamy.

"Here she goes," her father muttered, rolling his eyes.

"No one says courtship, Mom," Aspen grumbled. She couldn't help thinking of what the future would hold. Her and Declan's conversation in the car had seemed to address the elephant in the room, and she knew they would be fine.

The door to the bedroom opened, and a few seconds later, Declan appeared in the entryway to the living room.

"Is it safe to come in?" he asked with a hint of a smile on his lips.

"Of course it is," Mason replied, standing from the couch. He walked to Declan and reached out his hand. "I just want to officially thank you for everything you've done for our Aspen. That's my baby girl, and she's very special."

"It's an honor, sir." Declan nodded. His southern drawl was heavy as his eyes met Aspen's. "And I'd have to agree, sir. Now if you don't mind, I need to do something."

"Please, by all means." Her father waved Declan into the room.

Aspen glanced at her mother. Donna looked away immediately but not before Aspen could see the smile spread across her lips.

"What is going on?" she asked, suspicious of them all.

Declan walked across the room and knelt on the floor before her.

Her breath caught in her throat as she gazed into his eyes. "What are you doing?"

Her heart raced while he pulled a small black box from his pants pocket.

"Aspen," Declan began.

"Oh my God," she whispered. Her gaze flew to her parents and found wide grins on their faces. "Declan."

"We didn't start out with a conventional relationship," he said.

His eyes held hers, and she slowly forgot her parents were with them. This man before her, even though they'd only known each other for a short while, was the one for her.

Her parents had only dated for a couple of months before eloping, and it would seem she'd be following in their footsteps.

When the heart knows, the heart knows.

Who was she to question her heart?

Declan was hers, and she was his.

"Yes," she blurted out, thrusting her left hand out.

The room broke out in laughter.

"You don't even know—"

"Stop playing!" she hollered with a grin creasing her face. She danced around on the couch, excited.

"Marry me, Aspen," Declan asked, taking her hand in his.

"Yes, Declan. Yes!"

He pulled the large diamond ring from the black box and slid it onto her ring finger. It was a perfect fit. She flew forward, wrapping her arms around his neck.

"I love you so much," she cried out, gripping him tight.

"I love you, too," he murmured against her ear.

This day had to be the most perfect day of her life. She had reunited with her parents and had now just promised to spend the rest of her life with the man she loved.

EPILOGUE

Mac and Sarena's wedding reception was in full swing. As the best man, Declan was off duty. Mac and Sarena were officially married, and now it was time for him to snag a dance with the woman who had captured his attention the entire day. Sarena may have been a beautiful bride, but Declan's sights had been on Aspen.

The reception was held at an exclusive hotel in downtown Columbia. The ballroom was decorated with plush linens, silks, and endless amounts of flowers. Sarena had certainly outdone herself with the planning.

He strode through the crowd and searched the tables. He was sure Aspen would be sitting down. It had been months since the press conference, and now, after her intense physical therapy, she only used the cane for long distances.

His gaze landed on her sitting by herself. Music

blared through the speakers while laughter and drunk partiers sang to the popular song filling the airwaves.

Declan took his time walking over to Aspen. He drank in her dress that hugged her curves. It highlighted her deep cleavage, and Declan's mouth watered from the knowledge of what was hidden beneath it. The wine-colored dress brought out the smooth tones of her skin. Her feet, encased in low heels, tapped to the beat of the music. She tossed her dark hair over her shoulder, unaware of him approaching her.

His lips curved up in the corner while he watched her dance in her seat. The song morphed into a slow song.

Perfect.

"May I have this dance?" he asked, holding his hand out.

Her body jerked, and she swung around to him. A full grin spread across her face.

"Declan," she breathed, pushing her hair from her face.

"Come on," he encouraged.

"I don't know." Her brows dipped down in a frown. She glanced around the dance floor.

He could see the concern on her face and knew she yearned to be out amongst the dancers.

"Don't worry. I got you."

Her gaze turned back to him, and he switched on

his charm with a winning grin. The hesitation disappeared from her face as a smile spread across her lips.
"Trust me."

Her hand slid in his, and he pulled her from the
chair. He took notice she'd left her cane and allowed
him to tug her behind him to the dance floor. He
turned and drew her directly into his arms.

Exactly where she belonged.

She reached up and entwined her fingers at the
base of his neck. He eased her closer, leaving no room
between them. Her soulful eyes held his gaze, and he
found himself falling into the deep pools.

"The wedding was beautiful," she murmured.

"It was. I never thought I'd see the day Mac would
get married." He chuckled. "Did you see his face?"

"I think if Sarena would have been a few minutes
later, he would have gone searching for her." Aspen
giggled, laying her head on his chest as they swayed to
the slow song.

"I thought I'd have to cuff him to hold him still."
He laughed.

Sarena had been three minutes late, and that had
to have been the longest three minutes of Mac's life.
Mac was never one to have patience, and being made
to wait at the altar was almost a code red situation.

Later they found out it had been the flower girl
having to pee who'd held up the bride coming out.

"Well, let's just say they are perfect together."

"Yes, I'd have to agree." He breathed in her scent and gripped her tight, sliding his hand down to the curve of her ass. His cock stiffened, knowing it was close to Aspen.

"Declan," she whispered, pulling her head back.

She bit her lip, and it drove him crazy, wanting it to be his teeth on her plump lips. She looked around, but he already knew no one was paying them any attention.

"Why don't you take a walk with me." He squeezed her ass and laid a chaste kiss upon her lips. He couldn't wait until they got home. He was sure in the big hotel they could find somewhere to disappear for a short while. "I think there's something we need to go look at."

"Something to look at?" She cocked her perfectly sculpted eyebrow at him.

"Woman, just follow me."

She let loose a laugh and brought his head down to her. She pressed a hard kiss to his lips before pulling back. "Lead the way, Declan. I'll follow you anywhere."

THE END

A NOTE FROM THE AUTHOR

Thank you for taking the time to read Dirty Ballistics. I hope you enjoyed Declan and Aspen's story! If you love this book and want more from this series, please leave a review!

Reviews help authors know reader's reactions and that you want more from us! Thanks in advance!

Warm wishes,
Peyton Banks

ABOUT THE AUTHOR

Peyton Banks is the alter ego of a city girl who is a romantic at heart. Her mornings consist of coffee and daydreaming up the next steamy romance book ideas. She loves spinning romantic tales of hot alpha males and the women they love. Make sure you check her out!

Sign up for Peyton's Newsletter to find out the latest releases, giveaways and news! Click HERE to sign up!

Want to know the latest about Peyton Banks? Follow her online

ALSO BY PEYTON BANKS

Current Free Short Story

Summer Escape

Interracial Romances (BWWM)

Pieces of Me

Hard Love (Coming 2018)

Dirty Tactics (Special Weapons & Tactics 1)

Dirty Ballistics (Special Weapons & Tactics 2) (TBD)

Mafia Romance Series

Unexpected Allies (The Tokhan Bratva 1)

Unexpected Chaos (The Tokhan Bratva 2)

Unexpected Hero (The Tokhan Bratva 3)